The Mistress's Dog

14 May 2011

To Jayne and Martyn,

With very best wishes; and in appreciation, Jayne, of all you have done to promote South African literature.

Love, David

The Mistress's Dog

Short Stories
1996–2010

PICADOR AFRICA

First published in 2010 by Picador Africa,
an imprint of Pan Macmillan South Africa
Private Bag x19, Northlands
Johannesburg, 2116

www.panmacmillan.co.za
www.picadorafrica.co.za

ISBN 978-1-77010-174-6

Editing by Michael Titlestad
Proofreading by Louis Greenberg
Design and typesetting by Triple M Design, Johannesburg
Cover design by K4
Cover image by Dominic Morel

Printed by Ultra Litho (Pty) Ltd

Contents

For Karen Lazar, with my love

Acknowledgements

Michael Titlestad, who edited the manuscript of *The Mistress's Dog*, is the kind of editor every writer dreams of: generous yet exacting, precise without being dogmatic. My sincere thanks to him for his engagement with my stories and for writing the Foreword and Afterword.

Once more I am fortunate to have Picador Africa / Pan Macmillan as my publisher. I would like to thank Andrea Nattrass, Wesley Thompson, Terry Morris, Gerald de Villiers and all the team for their enthusiasm and the care they have devoted to my book. They should also be commended for their willingness to publish short stories (which are notorious for not selling well) during a difficult time in the publishing industry.

The writing group of which I am a member is a great joy in my life. It provides a loving and supportive environment in which creativity is nurtured and success delighted in. A big thank you to Darryl Accone, Maren Bodenstein, Emma Chen, Susie Dinneen, Damon Garstang, Liz Gunner, Kate Hutchings, Ellie Isserow, Jean Isserow, Jill

Nudelman, Shayleen Peeke, Geoff Sifrin and Renos Spanoudes.

I wish also to thank the following for their encouragement and useful suggestions: Elleke Boehmer, Molly Brown, Anthony Chennells, Isabel Hofmeyr, Karen Lazar, Elizabeth Leaver, Patrick Lenahan, Claudia Mitchell, Sharon Seftel, Ann Smith, Elena Thomas, Marijke van Vuuren, Andries Wessels and Fiona Wicksted.

* * *

Earlier versions of a number of the short stories in this collection have previously appeared in various publications. The author and present publisher would like to thank the editors and publishers concerned:

'Crowd Control' in *A Writer in Stone: South African Writers Celebrate the 70th Birthday of Lionel Abrahams*, eds. Graeme Friedman and Roy Blumenthal (David Philip, 1998);

'Free Range' in *At the Rendezvous of Victory and Other Stories*, ed. Andries Walter Oliphant (Kwela, 1999);

'The Mistress's Dog' in *New Contrast* (Vol.34, No.6, December 2006);

'Recognition' in *Running Towards Us: New Writing from South Africa*, ed. Isabel Balseiro (Heinemann, 2000); and *Encounters: An Anthology of South African Short Stories*, ed. David Medalie (Wits University Press, 1998);

'Toothless Tiger' in *New Contrast* (Vol.26, No.2, June 1998);

'The Tracks of Hidden Things' in *New Contrast* (Vol.29, No.3, Winter 2001);

'Tussenfontein' in *New Contrast* (Vol.36, No.3, September 2008);

'Under The Dragon's Tail' in *New Contrast* (Vol.28, No.1, Summer 2000); and

'The Wheels of God' reproduced by permission of Penguin Books South Africa, © David Medalie, in *A Writing Life: Celebrating Nadine Gordimer*, ed. Andries Walter Oliphant (Viking and Penguin, 1998); and *HerStoria* (Vol.4, No.3, December 1998).

Foreword

The twelve stories that comprise this volume are delicate. They are fine in texture, quality and construction, and draw subtle distinctions in thought and feeling. Delicacy, though, can also imply empathy, and David Medalie's writing evinces an exquisite awareness of the circumstances and feelings of others.

Each story presents a portrait of the subjectivity of a character contending with aspects of the past, and the challenges of crafting a future. The title story, 'The Mistress's Dog', for instance, traces Nola's quiet resignation to her husband's life-long infidelity, which was only ever punctuated by evanescent and private moments of self-assertion and retribution. She has, following the death of her husband and his mistress, been landed with the mistress's aging, leaky dog: a living, dying metonym for her life of compromised loss. This situation – expressing the subtle agonies of a 'small' life – sets the tone for the collection.

'Small', which describes an evolved politics of power and identity as it plays out in the relationship between two residents of the Horizon retirement home, raises explicitly this matter of scale. Resonating with the modest canvas of the genre – and the constraints facing its author in terms of plot, setting and action – this story captures how events, even 'small' events, can express worlds of meaning and consequence. One can lose all proportion, the story suggests, even on a small scale, and lives are no less in the balance.

'Toothless Tiger' captures – also at the scale of the domestic – another dynamic of power, in this case implicating gender and generation. It is a portrait of the triangle of a mother, Paula, her son, Tony, and her father, Marcus. Set during a game-park visit, the story examines the emergence of self-assertion, not just in Tony, who is verbally pounded by his grandfather – and who has to craft a space for a different form of masculinity from that to which he is being subjected – but also for Paula, who has to recognise the limited power of her father and the prospective independence of her son before she can bring herself to inform them that her cancer, previously in remission, has returned.

But the stories, for all their attention to the quiet inner and domestic lives of those formidably haunted by memory, also present a portrait of contemporary South African experience. Most tack between the private and the public, between the subjectivity of their characters and the social realities of our present, in ways that illumine a distinctly post-apartheid condition of suspension – of persistent and unresolved suspense.

In some respects – though it would hardly travel well – 'Tussenfontein' would have been another appropriate title for the collection. In that story, Libby, now relocated to Sydney, 'is famous for nostalgia'. She looks back on her life on the farm Tussenfontein with unblemished and uncomplicated celebration, even as she sings the praises of her utterly functional Australian present. She lives, in counterpoint to Sam's agonised sense of compromise, in the best of two worlds. Sam, whose life is diminished and compromised, has a very different relation to the past: he lives with a sense of loss, and little sense of any prospect of an enlivening future.

This sense of an in-between condition – which Harold, the protagonist in 'Crowd Control', who discovers solace in the apparent enclave of a Cape Town antique shop, experiences as living on a mezzanine – is trenchant. The optimistic transitional moment in South Africa, following the demise of apartheid in 1994 and consisting in efforts at reconciliation and historical redress, has been followed by a far worldlier, diminished set of prospects. In the post-apartheid dispensation, emigration, crime, xenophobia, and a largely unaddressed disparity in wealth have left many despondent and uncertain about the future – which remains nascent and inchoate, even as we celebrate the victory over the injustices of the past. Our own and the nation's history, as the award-winning story 'Recognition' suggests, will never be things we can simply put behind us.

'Free Range' and 'Indian Summer' are portraits of this suspension (and suspense). The first traces the efforts of one man to face up to the imminent threats in his world, particularly his determination to resist the wave of crime threatening to engulf his neighbourhood. The process he engages, which eventually fails, nevertheless affords Simon the opportunity to conceive of meaningful action, of moving towards something, rather than resigning himself only to an imprisonment by his fears. 'Indian Summer', the most economical story in a collection characterised by economy, is a portrait of a white couple on the verge of that defining post-apartheid experience – emigration. Laura, once their daughter-in-law, has to confront the impossibility of dissuading them from their course as they set off to become strangers. Neither Simon nor Laura can change the world – not even their small corner of the world. Both experience the currents of contemporary South Africa sweeping through their lives, and leaving them adrift.

Even these cursory descriptions suggest that Medalie's stories, which are notably modernist in their aesthetic, do not push through to resolution. They are hesitant and eschew anything programmatic or ideological. Instead, they edge us towards insights – as characters engage the compromised nature of their lives and the illogic of political and social transition – that are simultaneously profound and imprecise. There is always something potentially epiphanic at the horizon of characters' understanding: it remains blurred, though, its true power residing in being simultaneously eruptive and elusive.

It is unfortunate that South African short stories attract such a limited readership. They have long been a spine of South African letters, and the centrepiece of those literary journals and popular magazines that were vital to the development of our public literary sphere (five of the stories in this collection appeared originally in *New Contrast*, one of those journals whose importance cannot be overstated). I came away from reading these twelve stories with a renewed respect for the capacities of the genre, and a sense – which I address in the Afterword to the collection – that (modernist) short stories might be uniquely appropriate to our contemporary South African context and the contours of our experience.

But there is more to this volume than the individual stories it comprises. Not unlike the short-story collections of Ivan Vladislavić, the whole is more than the sum of its parts. Medalie's stories are a series of improvisations on a range of themes and literary motifs: but

The Mistress's Dog

The night wind tugged at the house and slammed against the windows. Nola drank a glass of dry sherry, ate honey nougat and slices of camembert on poppy-seed crackers, and watched TV. The mistress's dog lay on her lap, snoring and twitching. Once he looked up, gazing at her with milky eyes. Then he lowered his head again.

At half past ten she prodded him. 'It's time for final ablutions,' she said. 'I want to go to bed.' She picked him up and put him on the floor. Then she unlocked the patio door. The mistress's dog padded behind her, his nails making clicking sounds on the tiles in the passage. The wind had died down a little, but still pushed against them as they made their way down the steps and into the garden. The smell of the sea was strong. Above them loomed the dark mass of the mountain. The mistress's dog sniffed the damp paving-stones and stumbled against a pot-plant. 'Hurry up,' she said to him. 'It's cold.' After a while he lifted his leg against a fuchsia. 'Thank you,' she said. A dog barked in the distance. The mistress's dog barked in response, a shrill, reedy sound.

He made scratching movements in the grass with his back legs. Nola carried him indoors.

She fed him again. He spent a long time hunched over his plastic bowl, but ate little. Most of his teeth were gone. His diet, for the last five years, had consisted exclusively of soft food. He suffered from chronic halitosis – or, to be more accurate, others suffered from halitosis in him. There was nothing that could be done about it.

He slept in a basket – which had accompanied him when he flew from Johannesburg, seven years ago – at the foot of Nola's bed. He followed her to the bedroom and hopped into it. She read for twenty minutes and then switched off the light. The dog's sandpaper breath rose and fell in the darkness. Occasionally he whimpered – but whether in the gratification of a dream or the rasp of its disappointment, she could not tell.

Nola had always preferred cats to dogs.

The mistress was considered attractive according to the fashion of that time. But for Nola there was always too much of her – too much laughing, too much heartiness, too much peroxide, too many teeth. Nola's word for her was 'blowsy'. Sometimes she described her as 'blond and blowsy' because she liked the demeaning effect of the alliteration. At other times she just said 'blowsy', confident that the two syllables would hold sufficient scorn.

The mistress thought of herself as bold, daring, unconventional. And in the context of the poor, religious, rural family she came from, she was. She remained single, devoted herself to what she called her 'career' (she was a powerful man's secretary), and had an affair that endured for over a decade with a married man (that same powerful man). She bought a flat, bought a vermilion car, bought the advice of an interior decorator, bought elocution lessons, bought cookery lessons, bought Italian olive oil, bought crushed garlic, bought tickets to the ballet, bought the records of Callas and Caruso, bought sunglasses that resembled the ones Callas used to wear.

She severed all contact with her family. She never went to church. But in the unfettered darkness of night (the mistress was a chronic insomniac), she would sometimes weaken and, ashamed of her weakness, beg God to look indulgently upon her and at least understand her rebellions, even if He could not condone their sinfulness. She wanted God to know that she longed only to be free. She asked God to consider what it meant for a woman like her to have to live in the crimping South Africa of the 1960s.

The powerful man who was her boss and her lover saw her as spirited and strong. She excited him for seven years. She interested him for another five. Then she neither excited nor interested him. But Nola (who was married for over forty years to that same powerful man) sensed that the mistress, for all her bravado, was a fearful person. She understood that, although she presented herself as independent, flagrantly independent, she was in fact frightened of being alone, terrified – to the point of obsession – of abandonment.

Sometimes the mistress invited Nola and her husband to her flat for dinner and Nola would feel obliged to admire the food, the wine, the work of the interior decorator. She would pat the mistress's little dog. (There was a succession of small, yappy dogs over the years; the mistress was never without one.) But she preferred cats to dogs. And the food was always a little too oily, a little too salty, the wine too sweet, the flat too cluttered. Nola saw in the mistress the hesitation that the hearty laugh could not hide, the timorousness that was silent but present all the time, like a heart murmur. It was evident to her that the mistress had become a snob largely because she dreaded the judgement of snobs.

In everything she did and said, the mistress declared her determination to be free. She was, she believed, making and remaking herself. It was very hard work. It was expensive too. But it would be worth it if, by chipping away at herself, she could set herself free forever: a complete metamorphosis.

Nola knew, however, that the mistress had not even begun to emancipate herself. And she suspected that she never would. For she, Nola, was not free either, except from anxieties about money. She knew what the mistress had not yet discovered, which was that nothing grew in the shadow cast by the powerful man.

But it didn't make her sympathetic to the mistress's predicament. 'Blowsy,' she would say. 'Blond and blowsy.'

The next morning the sun shone, but the wind was cold. The mistress's dog, after performing successfully the first ablutions of the day, slept on a rug in the lounge, in a patch of sun. He was less wheezy than he had been during the night, but his breathing was shallow. He lay so still that whenever Nola walked past him, she bent over to see whether or not he was dead. But each time, she heard the tenacious little breaths, saw the rise and fall of the scrawny belly.

She would have liked him to die like that, during his sleep – not because she wished him gone, but because she lived in dread of having to have him euthanased. The vet was prepared to do it at any time: the mistress's dog, he said, was at least eighteen years old, almost toothless, almost blind, more than a little deaf, suffering from heart failure. She need have no qualms, the vet told her. It would be perfectly appropriate; even humane. But Nola couldn't bear the responsibility. She didn't want the needle to do its work at her prompting. She clung still to the hope that the life of the mistress's dog would end of its own accord. She didn't want to have to choose the moment of extinction, to say 'today is the day; now is the time'.

Was she keeping him alive, she wondered, simply because she was too cowardly to make that choice? Wasn't avoiding that choice a choice in itself? All her life, whenever she had had to make momentous choices, she had felt the pressure to choose as a weight that lay upon her, squeezing and stifling her. Sometimes she had chosen wisely, sometimes foolishly; but, whatever the outcome, the act of choosing had been in itself an agony.

The mistress's dog was old when he came to them; he would not live long, the powerful man had assured her. But he was wrong. The dog lived on in increasing decrepitude. And now it was not only his life for which she was solely responsible, it was his death too. Near the end of her life, when the anguish of having to make choices ought to be fading at last, the mistress's dog threatened her with the choices associated with his death.

It would be much, much better, Nola thought, if death would come to him there and then; if – with all the euphemistic kindness death is reputed to be capable of – it would gather him in as he slept in a patch of sun on a cold day.

Isn't that what we all want?

But it did not happen.

No one ever told Nola that her husband was having an affair. No one needed to. The powerful man's studied indifference towards a woman whom he so evidently admired, the excessive friendliness of that woman towards her, the gushing pretence that she desired a friendship to develop between them (it never did) – all these things told her unequivocally that the secretary had turned into the mistress.

Nola chose to say nothing. She allowed herself to be invited to the mistress's flat; occasionally, when she felt she had to, she invited the mistress to her home. But whereas the mistress would invite just the two of them, Nola and the powerful man, Nola always ensured that the mistress was invited to her home as part of a large dinner party. She selected the other guests carefully. They were always people the mistress had never met. They had old money. They had read old books. They had seen old paintings. They had visited old cities. They were soft-spoken. The mistress, in their company, became heartier than ever, as abrasive as a typewriter in a room in which people were writing on soft vellum with quills and ink. In the garrulous terror of the mistress, the resulting discomfort of the powerful man and the condescension of the soft-spoken people, Nola found a small but piquant revenge.

The mistress's dog woke up in the afternoon and went from room to room, looking for Nola. He found her in the entrance-hall, about to leave for the supermarket. 'I'll see you later,' she said, closing the door. He whined. Nola opened the door again and carried him to the car. 'Oh, all right,' she said.

In the car she rolled down the window a few inches. The mistress's dog pushed his face into the wind, his ears back and his tongue hanging out. He sneezed several times.

It was a day of clear light and cold blue skies. The supermarket was not far away; still, Nola found the trip arduous. Even when she kept to the speed limit, other motorists seemed to be annoyed with her for travelling too slowly. And when she backed into a parking-space, someone hooted at her – she was doing that too slowly too. A young man knocked against her as she walked into the shopping-centre and didn't even apologise. He was talking on a cellphone.

Nola pushed the trolley with one hand and held the mistress's dog in the other. He quivered against her arm. The honey nougat was on the top shelf. Nola put the dog down so that she could reach it more easily. She heard him make a little sound, almost as if he were sneezing again; but when she looked down, she saw that he had vomited on the shiny supermarket floor. The vomit was runny and yellow. 'Oh, no!' she said. 'Oh, no!' He looked up at her.

There was no one about – Nola could have crept away and slipped out of the supermarket, leaving the misdemeanour to be discovered later. But she did the right thing: she reported it and returned to the aisle, standing guard over the vomit, warning people not to tread in it. Eventually a young woman arrived to clean it up. She was sullen, resentful. 'I'm really sorry,' Nola said. 'I truly am.'

'You mustn't bring your dog in here,' the young woman said. She was big and her uniform was too tight for her. It strained against her as she bent down to clean up the mess. Her face, when she looked up, had a greasy sheen.

'You're right,' said Nola. 'You're absolutely right. I won't bring him here again. I promise.' She was as contrite as the circumstances demanded. But something also made her want to put in a plea, to soften this thick resentment. 'You know,' she said, as the young woman heaved herself to her feet, 'he's a very old dog. These things happen when you're old.' This produced no response. 'We all get old,' Nola said pointedly.

The face of the supermarket employee came perilously close to Nola's as she brushed past her. 'They must shoot me first,' she said.

Nola knew when the affair was over, just as she knew when it had begun. The mistress continued to work for the powerful man, but now she was just a secretary, no longer a mistress. When the powerful man retired, so did she, declaring she could not work for anyone else. She was loyal to the end, even though the clandestine days were long gone. And no doubt she envisaged a continued relationship of sorts with the powerful man: the succour of reminiscences, of anecdotes of the years spent together.

But the powerful man retired with Nola to the coast, to Cape Town (his idea, not Nola's); and the mistress remained in Johannesburg. She wrote, she phoned every week (expensive as it was); she did whatever she could to wring a last drop of solicitude from him. But all he gave was money. 'She's hard up,' he said to Nola. 'I must do what I can to help her. After all, she worked for me for over thirty years.' When she moved from her flat to a retirement village, he financed the move, for the cottage in the retirement village cost far more than she received from the sale of her flat.

Nola said nothing about the money, but she protested when the powerful man spoke to her (with unwonted awkwardness) of the mistress's dog – the current one, the last of the many small, yappy dogs.

'She can't take it with her to the retirement village,' he said. 'No pets allowed. Ridiculous, isn't it? You'd think they would realise that elderly people need the company of pets.'

'There must be someone else who can take it,' said Nola.

'There isn't.'

'Then she must ask the SPCA to find a home for it. Or have it put down.'

'It's an old dog. If she takes it to the SPCA, they will put it down. That will break her heart.'

'It's not my problem.'

'Please, Nola. It won't be for long. As I said, he's an old dog. He's on the way out.'

It was one of the few occasions in their marriage in which Nola had had the power, the absolute power, of decision. The choice was truly hers. If she had persisted in saying no, the mistress's dog would have remained in Johannesburg and, no doubt, would have been euthanased. It was an opportunity for revenge such as she had never had before.

But it had come too late. The powerful man had gout, an enlarged heart and a flickering memory. The mistress was no longer robust. They would never see each other again. It was too late, far too late, to triumph over them.

The mistress's dog was flown to Cape Town in a crate.

'I prefer cats,' Nola said when he arrived.

That night they sat once more in front of the TV. Nola drank dry sherry, ate honey nougat and slices of camembert on poppy-seed crackers. The mistress's dog lay on her lap.

'That was your last trip to the supermarket,' she said to him. 'Never again. No matter how much you cry.'

He bent his head towards her hand and licked it.

We are the survivors, she thought, the two of us. The powerful man had died in a Cape Town hospital after weeks on a ventilator. The mistress had died in the frail-care section of the retirement village in Johannesburg. The mistress's dog had outlived them both. And so had she.

Who would have thought that she would spend her last days with this ancient animal – with a dog that used to belong to her husband's mistress? Had she chosen him? Or had she ended up with him by default because she had not, during her life, made the wise, the adroit choices? If we are our choices, then what did it say about her that the mistress's dog was her last companion?

She sighed. He looked up at her with milky eyes. 'It's time,' she said, 'for final ablutions.'

Tussenfontein

The shadows stretch over the swimming-pool. The water is chilly on his skin as the afternoon retreats. He hears the sporadic beating of wings as, one by one, the guinea-fowl settle for the night in the bluegum trees.

'I still bake,' says Libby, 'but nothing tastes right any more.' She looks at Sam with those cloudy blue eyes that he has known since he was a boy. 'Maybe it's the butter,' she says, sighing. 'Or the flour. Or the eggs. It might even be the oven. I don't know. All I know is that it just doesn't come out as well as it used to when I baked everything in the old Aga stove at Tussenfontein.'

Whatever the topic, sooner or later Libby will make a loop back to Tussenfontein. Her conversation, on her annual visit to South Africa (Libby has been living in Sydney for fourteen years), is divided sharply between her new and old lives. Her new life is for informing: Sam, despite repeated invitations, has never been to Australia. Her old life is for reminiscing. In her presence, Sam returns to Tussenfontein, where he spent huge chunks of his childhood and adolescence, visiting Libby's sons, Danny and Wayne.

'Johanna and I were the only ones who knew how to get that stove going,' says Libby. 'Do you remember how temperamental it was? But we understood its moods. "Ons ken hom, Mis' Libby," Johanna used to say. "Ons ken hom. As ons praat, dan luister hy."' Libby likes to talk Afrikaans; she's proud that she still speaks it with a good accent. 'What roasts we used to make in that old stove!' she says. 'And what baking we used to do!'

Libby is famous for nostalgia.

Sam, however, has qualms. He understands the impulse to be nostalgic. When a smell or a song or a saying takes him back to something warm, he feels that Libby is wise. She knows that nostalgia is what helps us find our way back – that it's all we have.

But at other times, especially when the night wind is very cold, and the stars seem more than usually inhospitable, he's inclined to think that nostalgia is just a story we tell ourselves so that we don't have to admit that we will not be able to find our way back. And that's because we were never there in the first place.

With Libby, though, he has no choice. He can interact with her only on her own terms. And that means nostalgia unabashed. She knows no other way.

It's years since any of them have had anything to do with Tussenfontein. Libby sold the farm after her husband's early death – neither of her sons wanted to go farming. For decades they have all lived urban lives. But Libby's memories are rural. She lived in a townhouse in Johannesburg for twenty years, followed by fourteen in a flat in Sydney; but she'll always be a farmer's daughter and a farmer's wife.

'Spring is such a dry season on the highveld,' she says. She squeezes

Sam's hand and puts her arm in his. But Sam isn't sure whether it is the adult Sam, whom she sees once a year, of whom she is so very fond, or whether this is an overflow of the affection she felt for the young boy who used to come to Tussenfontein to play with her sons. 'Do you remember,' she says, 'how we used to wait for the first spring rains to soften the ground so that the ploughing could begin? You can't really expect rain before the tenth of October – what used to be Kruger Day. That's what my father used to say. Rain before the tenth of October is a pasella. But now it seems as if the spring rains come later and later every year. Even the weather is changing.' She sighs. 'When they abolished Kruger Day,' says Libby, making a rare joke, 'they abolished the rain.'

Sam remembers the arrival of the first rain: the dank, forgiving smell of it. He recalls the sudden emergence after the rain of the flying ants, their discarded wings lying like scraps of silver in the moonlight. Their short, frenzied lives used to distress him.

'Oh, and do you remember the thunderstorms at Tussenfontein?' asks Libby, squeezing lemon into her tea. She likes her tea with lemon and without milk. 'They were the most dramatic I've ever known. Sometimes the electricity would be out for days after a storm. But we could still cook and bake, thanks to the Aga.'

Libby is notorious for nostalgia.

But Sam notices that although she's full of love for the past, there's a curious absence of melancholy in her nostalgia. Her memories are not curdled by time and, although they speak of loss, they are not disfigured by it. They have been able to survive a widowhood when Libby was in her forties, her having to sell Tussenfontein, the move to Johannesburg, the emigration to Australia. Her memories are sturdy children.

Sam's are different. A dark thread is woven through them. He cannot slip in and out of the past, as Libby seems able to do. It tugs at him; it wants to hold him in an awkward embrace.

Libby never arrives empty-handed. She brings gifts from Australia, and, before she visits Sam in his flat, she bakes for him. She stays, on her annual visit to South Africa, with friends or relatives, and she uses their stoves, their kitchens. She presents Sam with the tastes of his childhood: meringues and lamingtons.

Tussenfontein: no one knows the origin of the farm's curious name. The names of other farms in the area are self-explanatory: Brakdam, Noukrans, Blinkpan, Stilgat. But Tussenfontein? What does it lie *between*? It doesn't feel like a between-place: during all the years of Sam's visits to the farm it feels to him as if everything starts and ends there. He can make no sense of it. Libby doesn't know what the name means either, nor does Uncle Arnold. (Libby's husband is Uncle Arnold to the English-speaking kids, Oom Arnold to the Afrikaans kids, but Libby, because she insists on it, is always just Libby to all the children. She has never been an Auntie or a Tannie.)

Whenever the boys emerge from the swimming-pool at Tussenfontein, Libby's meringues and lamingtons are waiting for them in the shade of the gazebo, covered with a white cloth to keep the flies away. The meringues are wispy and sticky in the centre; the lamingtons brushed with coconut, thick with dark chocolate.

Tussenfontein is the only farm in the district that has a swimming-pool. On his parents' farm, if he wants to swim, Sam has to make do with the reservoir, the sides of which are slippery with slime, the bottom too dark and deep ever to be seen. After you've swum in it, you have to shower to wash off the remnants of the greenish water. But

Libby has the bluest pool he's ever seen. The water tastes of chlorine, there is a pump which prattles away, and a lethargic Kreepy Krawly scours the bottom of the pool: as soon as they came on the market, Uncle Arnold bought one.

The farm has everything that farms should have: sheds and other outbuildings, tractors, combine harvesters, a dairy, horses and cows. But for Sam the heart of it is the swimming-pool. They swim until it is dark, he and Danny and Wayne. In the distance they can hear the sound of the milking-machines and a brief, sudden cacophony of indignant geese. Above them the first stars press through a violet sky.

Libby's memories are, of course, of the old South Africa. The New South Africa she knows only as a tourist. And she speaks of it as a tourist would – a disparaging, unimpressed tourist. 'How expensive things have become!' she says. 'I don't know how people manage, especially the elderly. In Australia they really look after their old folk. It's a very caring, humane society.' She looks out of the window. 'And the way you all live!' she says. 'In gilded cages. Look at these electrified fences. These security systems. I don't think I could bear it. On Tussenfontein we didn't even lock the doors of the farmhouse. And in Sydney I walk alone at night; I take public transport. I go wherever I want.' It's astonishing to Sam to see how rapidly she has transformed herself into an inhabitant of another country; how, within a relatively short time, she has learned to see South Africa from a distance, with the eyes of a visitor.

Sam discerns a curious paradox in Libby. She adheres more closely to origins than anyone he has ever known. She dwells on the past to such an extent that in some ways she may even be said to dwell *in* the past. Yet she has adapted with remarkable ease to a new country and a new continent. She was almost sixty years old when she emigrated – an age when many would baulk at such a grievous uprooting. And yet she seems to have had the smoothest of passages.

Sam tries to account for this. Perhaps, he thinks, Libby is able to face the present with equanimity because her relationship with the past is not a vexed one. For her it's like mourning the death of one whose devotion and loyalty have always been and will always be beyond question. There is loss, great loss, but there is no mistrust. Libby is enamoured of the past, but she isn't intimidated by it; nor is she suspicious of it. Sam wonders whether her nostalgia plays a part in that – whether it's her way of making the past docile. Or is it because Tussenfontein is sealed into her heart, perfectly preserved? Is she nourished by a dream so tenacious that it defies even the contradiction of passing days?

It never ceases to amaze Sam that, whenever Libby comes to South Africa, she sets time aside to pay a visit to Tussenfontein. She has no family members in that part of the world any more and very few old friends; and it must be heart-breaking to find other people living on the farm and in the house in which you grew up, and in which you spent all your married life. It would be understandable if she made every effort to avoid going there. But no: she visits the farm every year. She has even become friendly with the new owners, Mr and Mrs du Preez, who welcome her warmly, show her the improvements they've made, and receive gifts which she's brought all the way across the Indian ocean: a tablecloth one year, serviette-holders another. Everything says *Made in Australia*.

She tells Sam of the changes she has witnessed at Tussenfontein. 'The bluegum trees are simply *enormous* now,' she says. 'You remember how you used to be able to stand in the vlei and look up at the house? Well, you can't any more. You can't even see the house. It's completely obscured by the trees.' Libby walks to the window, turns around, returns to the couch. She always finds it difficult to sit still for long periods of time. Her movements are quick, decisive – even in their apparent aimlessness. 'Funny, isn't it, that there were always bluegum trees on Tussenfontein – and it never occurred to me to wonder whether they were indigenous or not. It didn't even cross my mind. And now I live in the country where they come from. They're Australian trees, and I never knew it.' She sits down, crosses her legs. 'Oh, and you remember the shed with the green door – the one beyond the dairy? It collapsed. There was a strong wind one day, and it just collapsed. Let me see – what else has changed? Oh, yes – the house has got burglar bars on all the windows. And they've closed in the stoep. Lettie du Preez tells me that she's learned how to shoot. She carries a gun in her handbag – a little silver one. She showed it to me.'

Sam doesn't know whether or not he should admire Libby for being able to return to Tussenfontein. Nothing would persuade him to return to any of the places he lived in as a child or a teenager. And although he didn't actually live at Tussenfontein, it feels to him as if it were one of his homes.

'Johanna is still alive,' says Libby. 'But she's almost blind now. "Hau," she said to me. "Mis' Libby, maar jy woon so *ver*!"'

Danny is a year older than Sam, Wayne a year younger. So he could be friends with either of them or with both. But Danny scorns his friendship, so Wayne, by default, is his friend. But Sam would prefer to be friends with Danny.

Libby's sons are adopted, so they don't resemble her or Uncle

Arnold or each other. Danny is tall and lithe and dark-eyed. His thick brown hair falls over his forehead, and he flicks it away with an habitual gesture. Wayne is skinny and pale and asthmatic. He wants nothing more than to be Sam's best friend, to make Sam replete with the satisfactions of his friendship. But it cannot be, for Sam is not even vaguely satisfied with Wayne's beaming, crestfallen attentions. He would like the haughty Danny to favour him, but there is no indication that that is ever likely to happen. He tries to talk to Danny and, while he's in the middle of a sentence, Danny turns away from him, dives, and does a full length underwater. When he resurfaces, he doesn't ask Sam to finish his story.

The first thing Sam discovers in Libby's swimming-pool is the cruelty of unequal affections.

The second thing he discovers is desire. One day – and it really is as sudden as that – he finds that it's not only Danny's attention or interest that he seeks. He is smitten, memerised by Danny's dark head, by his tawny neck, by the way he flicks his hair off his forehead, by his honeybrown torso and long legs.

One summer twilight they are all at the pool – Danny, two of his friends, Sam and Wayne. Danny's friends are thick boys, coarse and loud. Sam resents them. He cannot understand why Danny prefers them to him. He sits with the older boys, pretends that he's amused by their flaccid jokes. He hears Wayne calling him from the other side of the pool, but he ignores him.

Wayne runs towards the pool. 'Hey, Sam,' he says, 'let's ...' But he slips as he jumps in and hits his head on the side of the pool. There is a crunching sound that Sam hears for the rest of his life. He turns. Wayne, a small, white shape, lies face-down on the water.

The shadows stretch over the swimming-pool. The water is chilly on his skin as the afternoon retreats. He hears the sporadic beating of wings as, one by one, the guinea-fowl settle for the night in the bluegum trees.

Libby always brings photographs of Danny and his family, who also live in Sydney. Danny has an attractive blonde wife and three children. The children, as far as Sam can see, look very much like their father. But Danny no longer looks like Danny. Sam finds it disconcerting to see the fleshy face, the high, bald dome. There is nothing he can recognise of him in these photographs except the full lips and the imperious curve of the nostrils.

Libby, in the well-worn custom of grandmothers, brags about her grandchildren. They are athletic, musical, academically inclined, modest. 'I make meringues and lamingtons for them,' she says. 'Just like I used to make for you at Tussenfontein. But they don't taste as good. I don't know why.'

Libby has never attempted to justify her decision to emigrate. She has one son in Australia, one in South Africa. She could have stayed in Johannesburg. But she chose to go to Sydney. What it means is that she has chosen Danny, the son who emigrated to Australia, over Wayne, the one who stayed behind. Sam wonders whether it's because Danny has given her a daughter-in-law and grandchildren, while Wayne has not.

Wayne comes into the room. He is still thin, still pale. There is a large whitish scar on his forehead where it was gashed open that day at the swimming-pool. He suffers from migraines and seizures. He is vulnerable, diffident, almost unbearably gentle. He and Sam have been together for eight years.

Once again Libby urges Sam to visit her in Sydney. 'My flat is small,' she says. 'But there'll always be a bed waiting for you. Next time Wayne comes for a visit, you must come too.'

Sam isn't sure why he doesn't want to visit Libby in Sydney. After all, she's an utterly well-meaning and ever-affectionate embodiment of his past. And she's his present too: as Wayne's mother, she is, so to speak, his mother-in-law. But he doesn't know if he would be able to bear Libby's nostalgia in Australia. He imagines her reminiscing about Tussenfontein as she shows him her life in Sydney. And it seems to him like a double proprietorship, like a two-fold entitlement: Libby owning the new, just as she possesses the past. And he shrinks from it.

While Libby and Wayne lay the table, he goes out onto the balcony. The stars are as clear as they are ever likely to be in the city. People have named them and serenaded them and measured their distances. Yet it's one of those nights when they seem to shrink from him and all his kind. Anyone who looks at them, *really* looks at the stars, he thinks – as he has thought before – will not be nostalgic; will know that there are no returns and no enfolding days, nothing except an irredeemable between-ness and a high, wide dispossession.

He looks back and sees Libby bustling about, taking plates and glasses out of the side cabinet, bending over the table. And he feels a sudden surge of warmth towards her. He feels drawn to her tonight in all her simplicity and all her complexity.

If, as a species, we can't do without nostalgia, he thinks, then perhaps we should make a concerted effort to long only for places we have never actually been to. The top of Kilimanjaro, for instance. He has seen photographs of the grey shale, the great blocks of ice, Uhuru Peak. It's as cold and eerie as being on the moon.

He will live and die without making the ascent; therefore he can be nostalgic for the summit of Kilimanjaro.

Libby and Wayne both look up, smile at him as he re-enters the room. 'I'm not going to let up until you come and visit me in Sydney,' says Libby. 'Wayne has promised to help me persuade you.'

'One day,' says Sam. 'One day I'll surprise you and just turn up.'

'I can guarantee you one thing,' says Libby. 'Some of that old Tussenfontein hospitality.'

Small

Let us not take it for granted that life exists more fully in what is commonly thought big than in what is commonly thought small.

Virginia Woolf: 'Modern Fiction'

At night, when the ticking of the clock reaches into every corner of the darkened room, Stella lies motionless but awake. These are the hours which she dreads.

Why, she wonders, has sleep shunned her all her life? She remembers how, even as a child, she couldn't sleep properly. She would hear her parents' voices in their bedroom, and, later, her father's snoring. All the house would come to rest – except for her, alone in her struggle. It has always felt to her as if sleep were a sweet conspiracy in which she has no part. And so she's doomed to remain a pariah, her eyes rough with longing.

Stella has always had to make do with small.

It's not what she would have chosen. It was foisted upon her.

There was a weighty thing, a block of pure consequence, that was meant to come her way. But it never arrived. And now, as she ages, her life grows ever smaller. And instead of being resigned to it – elderly people are supposed to be adept at resignation – she's as indignant as a victim, as peevish as an overlooked child.

She lives in a retirement village called Horizon. She's acquainted with all the residents, at least by sight. She exchanges greetings with many of them. They make a lot of small talk. Most of the residents know the bald facts of her life: she was a hospital administrator for many years, never married, has no surviving family.

But in knowing that, they know nothing.

She lives there quietly for four years. And then suddenly everything changes: one of the residents dies, a cottage becomes available, and Gwen moves in. Before she's even aware of what's happening, Stella finds that Gwen has appropriated her. She's caught in a friendship that she doesn't want. And having permitted it at first, she doesn't know how to stand up to Gwen now or distance herself.

Life has treated Gwen well, but this hasn't made her grateful; instead, it has made her feel entitled. Having had so much for so long, she has no qualms in demanding even more – unlike Stella, who demands nothing, except in her tight-lipped fantasies.

She knows that Gwen isn't popular amongst the Horizon residents, and that her association with her means that they're avoiding her too. She overhears people speaking disparagingly of Gwen, calling her 'overbearing', even 'impossible'. And Stella thinks how unjust it is that she, who has never borne over anything or anyone, who has always been too possible for her own good, should be shunned along with Gwen. And the irony is that, as far as she can tell, Gwen is too thick-skinned to realise how people feel about her. She knows that she doesn't mix much with the other residents, but she doesn't seem to be aware that she's being slighted. It's Stella who sees it. And the more the others avoid her, the more she's forced to spend time with Gwen.

Vicious circles are always small.

Gwen never visits her; she has to visit Gwen. Stella's flat in the retirement village is a bed-sit: bathroom, tiny kitchen, bedroom and sitting-room combined. It was all she could afford. She has an armchair and a wooden chair with a straight back next to her bed; if more than two people come to visit, she has to sit on the bed. But very few people visit, so it's not a problem. She's not dissatisfied with her bed-sit: there's something about it which reiterates the course of her life. If nothing else, it's an honest home.

Gwen, who is not short of money, has a large cottage – almost a house. It has its own garden and footpath, two bedrooms, a lounge and a dining-room. It's uncomfortably furnished because Gwen, who moved there from a mansion in Dunkeld, was loath to give up her belongings, so she squashed heavy furniture into rooms that, although spacious, are not big enough for such grand pieces. As a result, her cottage reminds Stella of a furniture salesroom – a very upmarket one, but a salesroom nonetheless. Of course, she would never intimate that: her job is to admire and to congratulate.

If Gwen were ever to think of things in terms of big and small – not that she *would*, of course – Stella knows that she would not hesitate to assert that her life has been big: bulky with the gratification of monumental days. The years, as she reviews them for Stella, are stuffed with satisfaction. She tells Stella over and over about her husband, the mining engineer, the double-storey house, the terraced garden, the huge dinner parties she hosted, the servants dressed to welcome the guests in cummerbands and white gloves, the ice sculptures, the violin quartets, the Mediterranean cruises, the rose propagated in her honour and bearing her name: Gwennie's Pride (her husband always called her Gwennie). 'It's a deep, deep pink,' she says. 'The ones I planted in the garden here didn't make it. But I must try again, so you can see what it looks like. Quite the loveliest pink you've ever seen.'

In the garden of Gwen's cottage and on the stoep, in terracotta pots, there are new shrubs and flowers. But although she spent a lot of money, the garden doesn't look good. Gwennie's Pride was not alone in dying almost immediately, and even those plants which survived seem to be struggling. Gwen attributes it to the poor soil, but Stella thinks there's something else that turns the leaves yellow and makes the buds drop unopened to the ground.

Gwen drops names all the time, mostly of rich and prominent people. Stella is scornful of what she considers to be lamentably poor taste: bragging about wealth and social importance; but occasionally, despite herself, she's a little impressed. However shallow Gwen's life must have been, at least it was busy with ambition and activity. Or was it? She has her doubts. These important people can't all be dead, yet they don't visit Gwen in the retirement village. And it seems to her that if she listens carefully when Gwen speaks, she can sometimes discern a timorous note, something that falters, that can't quite reach the crescendo of its own self-satisfaction.

And there is this to consider: if you have truly lived a big life, do you *need* to drop names?

Even Gwen cannot pretend that her present life is large. Nothing can hide the fact that she's an elderly widow, living in a cottage in a retirement village. But her response is to construe increasingly hyperbolic fantasies of importance within the social hierarchy of the retirement village. Her isolation, she declares, is evidence of the awe in which she's held: people know who she was, who her husband was, and are intimidated.

Stella thinks of an epithet that sums Gwen up perfectly: *she gives egomania a bad name*. It comes to her during one of the long, sleep-evading nights. She's proud of herself for devising something so clever and witty. But she has no one to share it with. She never, ever criticises Gwen to any of the other residents. For better or for worse, their lives are so intertwined that for her to say what is nothing but the truth, to disparage in Gwen that which no one would blame her for deprecating, has become, by some curious twist of circumstance, an act of disloyalty towards herself.

On the sideboard in the dining-room are photos of Gwen's family: she and her husband, Terence, on their wedding-day, Terence dressed in a tuxedo, standing next to the then Administrator of the Transvaal ('He became a family friend,' says Gwen, 'almost an intimate of ours. That educated type of Afrikaner is a pleasure to mix with'), Gwen being presented with Gwennie's Pride shortly after it was propagated ('Quite a thing,' she says, 'to receive a rose grown specially in your honour. I told you, didn't I, that afterwards they made it into a creeper too?') Most of the photos, though, are of Vernon: as a baby, a schoolboy, playing cricket, graduating from university ('*Cum laude*,' says Gwen), getting married, playing with his children.

Vernon is Gwen's son, her only child. He's forty-three years old, lives in Cape Town, is a maxillo-facial surgeon, married with three children. Stella has never met him, but she dislikes him intensely. Even his name annoys her. She knows that, logically, he can't be blamed for something he didn't choose, but there is a sense in which he can be held responsible for it, for he seems to have dedicated his life to achieving the pomposity his name promised him. In the photographs he looks unbearably pleased with himself, his lips curled in condescension, reaching for a smirk. His wife is always pictured looking adoringly up at him; his children are shown clamouring to be embraced by their father, to be hoisted onto his shoulders.

Fortunately, he has not yet been to visit Gwen in Horizon. 'Vernie's so busy,' says Gwen. 'It can take up to six months to get an appointment with him. His patients think the world of him, you know. He phones me every single day – never forgets, no matter how busy he is, even when he's overseas. The other day the phone rang and he said, "Guess where I am? In Louisville, Kentucky. Attending a medical conference." He begged me to come and live in Cape Town when Terence died, said he would build a cottage onto his house in Camp's Bay, but I didn't want it. I'm a Transvaler through and through – or whatever the Transvaal's called now. Lived here all my life. Rain in the winter would drive me dilly.'

Stella doesn't believe any of this. Vernon, she feels, could have made time to visit his mother and see her new home, no matter how busy he is. And he has never phoned while she's with Gwen, so when do these daily calls take place? But that doesn't redeem him in her eyes. Even if he has the good sense not to be fond of his mother, he's still fallen victim to the reprehensible family malady: he's enamoured of himself. One can see it in every photograph. Gwen clearly has the son she deserves.

One morning she's summoned to visit Gwen earlier than usual. She tries, uncharacteristically, to resist: she has a headache and wants to lie down. But Gwen is insistent. 'Something's happened,' she says, 'I must talk to you.' When she arrives at the cottage, Gwen seizes her by the arm and pushes her towards a chair. 'This is between you and me,' she says. 'Strictly *entre nous*.'

'Of course,' says Stella. Gwen's injunction is redundant: she would never repeat anything that passes between them.

Gwen looks agitated, even a little dishevelled: her hair, which usually rises in stiff waves like a frozen sea, seems to have collapsed in the middle. She sits down and then jumps up again. 'This has never happened,' she says. 'Never.'

'What has …' Stella begins to ask.

Gwen interrupts her, begins to speak, then stops. Finally she gets it out. Stella, when she gathers what has happened, is astonished that such a fuss should be made.

Vernon's marriage has collapsed.

'Is that *all*?' Stella is about to retort, but stops herself. 'It's certainly very sad,' she says instead, 'but you can't say it has never happened. Unfortunately, it's all too common. Many marriages don't work out. Despite the best of intentions.'

'Not in *our* family,' laments Gwen. 'We've never had any divorces. Never been associated with any scandal.'

'Scandal? It's upsetting, I know, but where's the scandal?'

Gwen, however, will not allow the tragedy to be mitigated. More details emerge: Vernon's wife has been having an affair, and it is she who wants the divorce. Her lover lives in Johannesburg; she's leaving Cape Town and moving up to Johannesburg, to be with him. The children are going with her. Vernon cannot give up his practice, and so the children will have to fly down on alternate weekends, and he will have to come up from Cape Town on the other weekends to see them. Gwen makes much of the unfairness of it all: Vernon has done nothing wrong, he is the injured party, and yet he will have to be parted from his children during the week, and pay for all these plane trips, not to mention the monthly maintenance costs (his wife's demands are, predictably, exorbitant, and will have to be challenged in court).

Stella says the right things, but in her heart she can find no compassion whatsoever. Something small intrudes, a worm of meanness, and it makes the news perversely thrilling. She can't help it. The idyllic family turns out not to be idyllic after all. The adoring wife was anything but adoring. More than a marriage has collapsed: what lies in ruins is the edifice that complacency built. How can she not take pleasure in that?

Gwen requires much consoling in the weeks that follow. Stella, who feels a little guilty about tolerating – even nourishing – the worm of meanness, tries to be as attentive as possible. 'What did I do to deserve this?' Gwen asks again and again. It's impossible to tell her that this is a dispute between a man and his wife; that it has nothing to do with her.

Vernon begins his fortnightly visits to Johannesburg, and he usually includes a visit to his mother after he has returned the children to his estranged wife. He comes for tea on Sunday afternoon, before he leaves for the airport. Stella would like to meet him, if only to witness first-hand his deflation, but at first there's no opportunity to do so. Gwen is jealous of the short time spent with him, and does not wish to share him with anyone. But one day a niggardly invitation is issued: 'Vernie would like to meet you,' says Gwen. 'I told him it's not necessary, but he wants to. Anyway, you don't have to stay long.'

As Stella enters Gwen's lounge on that Sunday afternoon, a tall man stands up and makes his way towards her with outstretched hand. Stella is puzzled: surely this can't be Vernon? It's as if the features of the man in the photographs have been transposed onto another face. There's no trace of the smugness or hubris which she has long despised. The smile is broad, the skin around the eyes crinkles as he smiles, and the eyes themselves are a warm brown. As he shakes Stella's hand, he clasps it in both of his. 'I've been looking forward to meeting you, Stella,' he says. 'I know what a good friend you've been to my mother. I want to thank you.'

'Nothing to thank,' mumbles Stella. 'I've done little enough.'

'You haven't,' Vernon says, guiding her to a chair. 'You've been wonderful. You've given tremendous support.' He's gallant without being stiff.

Gwen sniffs as she reaches for the teapot. 'I'm not one for wearing my heart on my sleeve,' she says. 'All my life I've stood on my own two feet.'

As she lowers her head to pour the tea, Vernon turns to Stella. He raises one eyebrow. Then he winks at her – a slow, deliberate wink.

And in that moment of the wink, everything changes.

Now she counts the days until every second Sunday afternoon. Gwen, after the first meeting, tries to prevent further encounters, declaring them unnecessary, since Stella and Vernon have now met. But Vernon makes it clear that he wishes Stella to be invited every time he visits and his mother is forced to give in. And, in any case, Stella simply turns up: nothing Gwen can do or say will keep her away. She watches until the car is parked outside Gwen's cottage (always a different one – Vernon picks up a hired car at the airport), and, after giving the son and mother no more than ten minutes alone together, she walks across. Gwen glares at her, but she pays no attention.

Vernon is clearly pleased to have her there. He's seeing much more of Gwen than he has for years, and, he confides to Stella, he finds it a strain. It helps to have someone else to talk to. Occasionally he brings the children with him, but more often he's alone. The children's visits to their grandmother are a conspicuous failure: they're bored and listless, taciturn to the point of discourtesy, and they look at their watches all the time and send messages on their cellphones. Even Gwen cannot pretend to be enthusiastic about seeing them. 'It's understandable,' she says. 'They're at an awkward age. Most of them go through that phase. Except Vernie. He was never like that. He was always as sweet and gentle as he is now.'

Stella mistrusted Gwen's accounts of her son before she met him; now that she knows him, she's convinced that the Vernie who has been presented to her has never existed. Gwen has a son finer than anything she could construct in her mind, but she doesn't know him at all. The territory she defends so assiduously is a barren land, chilled by shadows of delusion. Stella's almost tempted to feel sorry for her, but she cannot. She and Gwen have become rivals and, in a contest so fierce and so bitter, compassion has no place.

Slowly, as if by mutual consent, the two women see less and less of each other. Gwen seldom summons Stella: she doesn't seem to feel the same need to talk to her. And Stella in turn keeps away. The ties that bound her to Gwen are loosening; and it is Vernon who has made that possible, who is freeing her from a suffocating friendship from which she had been unable to extricate herself.

But she never fails to turn up for tea on alternate Sunday afternoons.

By a tacit agreement, the fading of the friendship is hidden from Vernon. He believes that the two women are as close as ever and that the daily visits still take place. Stella encourages that belief because she doesn't want him to think that she's neglecting his mother. She's come to realise that Vernon is, after all, a good son, although he isn't, as Gwen always tried to suggest, doting: he finds his mother trying, but her welfare is nevertheless important to him. She discovers that he does indeed phone Gwen regularly – not every day, but several times a week, and always in the evening, which is why Stella has never been present when his call comes through. His solicitude is not affectionate, but it is sternly dutiful.

It puzzles her, though, that Gwen doesn't indicate to him that she's no longer as friendly with Stella as she used to be. It would be an opportunity for her to triumph over Stella by exposing her as an inadequately attentive friend. But she doesn't do so. Stella decides that it's because Gwen has a history of failed friendships and she wants Vernon to think that she's capable of keeping this one going. She needs him to believe in her as someone who can inspire loyalty – she needs that even more than she needs to keep Stella away from him. At this age she's still trying to win the approval of her middle-aged son.

The other residents notice the change in the relationship. 'Aren't you so friendly with Gwen?' one of them asks.

'No, I suppose not,' Stella replies. 'Well, we're still friends,' she adds hastily, 'but we don't feel the need to see each other every day any more.'

Once she has made this admission, the residents of Horizon become noticeably more cordial towards her. They begin to invite her to their homes for tea; they ask her to go shopping with them, or to the movies. She accepts, gladly. She's delighted by these overtures. But her gratitude is reserved for Vernon: it is he who has made these changes possible. He gives, she thinks, without even knowing that he gives.

As the months go by, Stella feels that in the contest between her and Gwen, she's prevailing. Vernon turns frequently to her, seeking her opinion. Sometimes he speaks to her in Gwen's presence as if his mother weren't there. He confides in Stella, telling her about his impending divorce, the greed of his ex-wife, her manipulation of the children, the vast fees claimed by the lawyers. 'Some things shouldn't go beyond the family,' says Gwen, looking pointedly at her son. 'There's no need for us to wash our dirty laundry in public, Vernie. Your father was very strict about that.'

Vernon asks Stella about her life and seems genuinely interested. At first she's reluctant to tell him much: she feels ashamed of the stunted years that have passed. She doesn't know how to explain to him why they never flourished. But he listens and encourages her and even the most mundane details don't seem to make him recoil. And so she grows less hesitant and tells him more. She notices Gwen gazing at her with astonishment, for in all the months of their friendship, their daily interactions, she never spoke of these things. Even if she'd wanted to, she would never have been given the opportunity. She revels in Gwen's amazement. She discovers what it feels like to have the tables turn in her favour. It's an acrid taste, strong but not unpleasant. 'It was always about you,' she would like to say to Gwen. 'It was never about me. But Vernon is making it about me. And there's nothing you can do about it.'

One day Gwen interrupts her sharply. 'We've all had our disappointments,' she says. 'We've all come down in the world. Look at me. Look what I'm reduced to. You never saw the house in Dunkeld, Stella. It was the epitome of gracious living.' She turns to Vernon. 'Am I right?' she asks.

'I suppose so,' he says. 'Although it became a bit dilapidated in later years. Those old houses are a nightmare to maintain. If you'd stayed there, you would have had to rewire the entire place. Probably redo the plumbing. And the roots of those old trees were destroying the driveway.'

Gwen glares at him. Then she struggles to her feet. 'Excuse me,' she says.

'Where are you going?' asks Vernon.

'Where no one can go for me.'

While she's out of the room, Stella leans towards Vernon. She feels anxious. This will be the great test of their friendship, the ultimate determinant of where his loyalty lies. 'I sometimes think ...' She stops. 'No, never mind.'

'What? Tell me.'

'You may take offence. She is your mother, after all.'

'*Tell* me.'

'I sometimes think ... wouldn't say it to another soul, of course ... I sometimes put it this way to myself ... she gives egomania a bad name.'

Vernon throws his head back. He laughs. He slaps his thighs. 'That's fantastic,' he says. 'I must remember that.' He laughs again. 'It will be our little joke. You *are* funny, Stella.'

Stella sits back, delighted. Her daring has paid off – more richly than she could have hoped. It has brought her and Vernon even closer. It has shown that they are truly allies.

When Gwen returns, Stella notices that she's not walking well – she shuffles and seems unsteady on her feet. And when she reaches for a cake plate, her beringed hand trembles. Stella feels a brief remorse. Gwen suddenly seems frail, deserving of her compassion. But she can give her none. The secret compact with Vernon is too important to her. If she needs to sacrifice Gwen to maintain it, then that's how it must be. The penury of the spirit under which she has suffered means that compassion is a luxury she cannot afford. She's too greedy to spare Gwen even a scrap of the repast which has come to her so late in life. She has waited too long for this to be distracted by qualms.

It is winter and Stella lies awake in the chilly darkness of her bedroom. The questions she banishes from her mind during the day force themselves upon her at night. Listening to the ticking of the clock, she tries in vain to fend them off. They are simple to pose, but very difficult to answer.

What do I truly want from Vernon?

Does my relationship with him have a future?

If so, what is it?

She finds that she cannot articulate her desires, even to herself. She's less afraid of what she yearns for than of the longings that she will not even permit, for the fantasies that have waylaid her since she met Vernon are, at their heart, diffident. One hope she cherishes, for instance, is of a lasting friendship with Vernon, one that will never fade. Another is that he will visit Horizon with the sole purpose of seeing her, Stella. Yet another is that she should become his chief confidante, entrusted with even more than the confidences that have already come her way.

It's not that she wouldn't like more. She sees him vividly before her as she lies in the dark, trapped in that sour marshland where those who cannot sleep live out their exile. She sees him wink at her, sees the way he throws his head back when he laughs. She sees the fine blond hairs on the back of his hands, the way he crosses his long legs, the beautiful leather shoes, always polished, never scuffed, he wears even on a Sunday. She smells his aftershave in the darkness of her bedroom – a room he has never entered.

She would like more, but she cannot begin to hope for it. There is not a chance that Vernon will fall in love with her. It's not only beyond the bounds of everyday possibility – it lies even beyond the reach of dreams. He can never desire her as she desires him. He's full of affection, of respect, of deference, but that's as far as it goes – as far it will ever go. To imagine more, even within the tight silence of clandestine longings, is to permit dreams that are absurd even to her.

And so she does not know what fantasies to feed in the dark, sleep-evading hours, for even a fantasy cannot be entirely free of curtailment. She lies there doing battle not only with what she longs for but cannot have, but also with what she does not dare to long for.

The smallness of her life is bad enough. Much, much worse, she finds, is the smallness of her dreams.

The idea of saving someone's life has always appealed to Stella. In that one, pure, definite act her own life, she has always believed, would find its validation and its piquant purpose. It would become its own justification. It would never feel small again. And so now, faced with fantasies that die even before they are born, she fantasises instead about saving someone's life. She decides that the life she will have to save is Gwen's. In the vision, as it plays itself out in her mind, she's at home one afternoon when, intuitively, she knows that something is wrong. Rushing over to the cottage, she finds the front door open and Gwen prostrate on the floor, almost unconscious. (Is she bleeding? Did she fall and knock her head? The details are not important.) She phones for help and Gwen is taken away on a stretcher. She pulls through and recovers her health. Vernon is deeply grateful to Stella; he knows his mother's faults, but, ever the dutiful son, he does not wish to lose her. In his indebtedness towards Stella, she secures his friendship forever.

For in the happiness of her present friendship with Vernon one terrible fear persists: that Gwen will die and that he will then disappear from her life.

The fantasy appeals to her for another reason too: she has been feeling increasingly guilty about her treatment of Gwen. It must pain her to witness the alliance between Stella and Vernon. Even she cannot be blind to the fact that there is an ease and a jocular warmth in their relationship that she does not enjoy with her own son. As things stand, Stella cannot assuage her guilt, for she will do nothing to jeopardise the intimacy between herself and Vernon. She sacrifices Gwen to secure her own happiness, and she does it with a ruthlessness which she recognises but will not temper. But in saving Gwen's life she would make amends to her and benefit herself all at once. It's the ideal scenario.

Best of all, saving Gwen's life is a fantasy which lies entirely within the bounds of possibility. As time passes, Stella begins to expect it. Gwen is not robust: she must fall ill. She must collapse and be brought back to health. She must succumb to illness but not die. And it is Stella – who but Stella? – who must save her.

It surprises Stella how the friendship with Vernon has altered even the way she looks back on her life. The frustrations and disappointments are still there – nothing can take them away – but they have a sharper focus, as if they lie now in direct sunlight. The shadows have disappeared. There is no longer any wistfulness. Her insomnia remains, but even the sleepless hours seem different to her now. Before they were her combatants, foes that would defeat her if she did not vanquish them; and, all too often, it was they who triumphed. But now there is an uneasy truce. She lies awake, but not with the same feeling of urgency. She hears without panic the first twittering of the birds and sees without anguish the grey light of the approaching dawn.

And if, as she lies there, she reviews her life, it is without self-recrimination. For who is there, she asks herself now, who has not led a small life? Are not all our lives tiny in comparison to the great cosmic maw which has spewed them out and will suck them back in?

Vernon has made it possible for her to be kinder towards herself. And in this new and unfamiliar peace she resolves to visit Gwen more frequently, to treat her better, to refrain from overt demonstrations of her victory.

Some weeks later, Stella's fantasy comes to pass, but only partially: prophetically true in many of its particulars, but entirely wrong in others. It fails her in its essentials: a grotesque inversion of what should have been.

It is late winter, a Sunday afternoon, and she makes her way to Gwen's cottage. She has no sense that anything is wrong. She walks slowly, enjoying the sunshine and admiring the jasmine, which is already beginning to flower. The gardens at Horizon are beautiful, she thinks, and so much care is given to looking after them. She has not appreciated them as fully as she ought. She's lucky to live here.

She turns the corner and Gwen's cottage comes into view. She stops. She gasps. She has imagined the scene so often that as it appears before her now it assumes a strange, beckoning familiarity. It's as if the desire and the reality are meeting in a curious, jolting dance.

The door of Gwen's cottage is open. The ambulance is parked at the end of her footpath. It is stationary although the red light is flashing. Two men are carrying a stretcher, while a nurse hovers near them, directing them.

An ambulance has come to Gwen's cottage, as she knew it would. But it is not she who summoned it: she's the onlooker, the late and incidental arrival, not the saviour.

And it is not Gwen on the stretcher, for she appears at the door of her cottage, her mouth open in silent distress, her arms raised.

The person being borne into the ambulance is Vernon.

At times it feels as if what has happened is so devastating that it will wipe out every sadness that Stella has ever experienced. But at other times it seems more like the culmination of everything that has ever made her unhappy, as if her life were a long apprenticeship in loss and now, only now, is her training to be put to the test.

The hours of lying awake at night are filled now with a futile struggle against grief. It's an underwater cavern into which everything flows and, borne along by the current, she too must enter the dark mouth. It is so big, and she so very small, that she can never emerge from it again.

Vernon, after being admitted to hospital in Johannesburg following the seizure, is transferred to Cape Town; and, while further tests are being done, Gwen goes to Cape Town too. Stella goes to her cottage to help her pack, but finds that she has already left. She cannot decide whether she misunderstood when Gwen's flight was leaving, whether Gwen mistakenly gave her the wrong information – or whether it was deliberate.

The diagnosis is not made known to her by Gwen, but by one of the other Horizon residents.

'Terrible news, isn't it?' the woman says to her, pausing as they pass each other on the footpath on the way to the administration block. 'About Gwen's son.'

'Yes,' says Stella, not wanting to admit that she knows nothing.

'She must be devastated,' the woman continues.

'She must be. I mean, she is.'

'And there's nothing they can do. They can't even operate.'

'Apparently not.'

'How long do people live?' Stella does not answer. The woman bends to scratch her leg. 'You know, with inoperable brain tumours,' she continues, looking up again. 'How long do they live?'

'I have no idea,' says Stella, turning away.

'Such a young man,' the woman calls after her. 'In his forties, I think.'

It strikes Stella one day that in all the time Gwen has been away, no one has been watering her plants. She takes her own watering-can and walks to the cottage. There's a cleaning-woman who comes twice a week, but Gwen has never trusted her with a key, so she's been unable to go inside the cottage during her employer's absence. Stella, too, doesn't have a key, so there's nothing she can do for the indoor plants. But she waters the ones on the stoep. They're wilting, but not dead yet – she's come just in time to rescue them.

As she walks to the tap and back, filling the watering-can, she has an unexpected reaction to Gwen's plants. She used to see their reluctance to thrive as a comment on their owner, on the poverty of her pretensions. But now, looking at the struggling plants again, she finds them deeply affecting. They're full of pathos, not of judgement. How is it that she never saw it before?

As she stands there with the watering-can still in her hand, a mood different from that of the previous days settles upon her. At first she's unable to identify it. But then it becomes clear to her: in the sorrow of the dusty plants there lies also the sorrow of Gwen – something she has scarcely considered since Vernon's seizure.

The bedraggled plants speak to her of a suffering that is no smaller for not being her own. Her own tragedy seemed so huge that it stretched from horizon to horizon. And so it is: the biggest thing ever. But she feels also how small – a pillbox, embossed with mother-of-pearl – is the receptacle in which have been gathered all her private and engrossing griefs, her solitary and tender disappointments.

When Gwen gets back from Cape Town, she will need a friend. More specifically, she will need compassion.

On the morning of Gwen's return, Stella awakes and is amazed to find that a lengthy period of oblivion has passed. Her sleep the previous evening has been deeper and sounder than any she can remember. Is it, she wonders, the start of something new? Or merely a respite?

Whatever it is, she's grateful to have had it. She savours the repose, even after it has ended. It was a minute, one small minute, redeemed from a stringent hour.

Free Range

Simon was a man who took care. His parents and his brother had all died before they were sixty-five and he had no intention of following them to what he considered an unacceptably early grave. Being an atheist, he had no hopes of an afterlife; all the more reason, then, to remain alive as long as possible, before oblivion put an end to it all. Longevity was Simon's earnest ambition. He became strategic about his lifestyle and diet. He would buy only the meat and eggs of free-range chickens and he never ate the skin. Red meat was out of the question. Biltong he considered to be nothing less than salted suicide. He avoided dessert for so long that eventually he came to believe that it was only for greedy people and so his objections to it became moral. As he grew older, life seemed to him more and more a matter of fending off dangers.

Simon always advised people to choose their parents carefully if they wanted a long and healthy life – it was his favourite joke. The poor generic inheritance which his parents had handed on to him had not spared his brother (who was younger than he), but Simon was adamant that there would be no determinism in his genes, only redemptive possibilities. He set what he was born with against himself as an antagonist. His efforts met with success. He began to look upon his dead brother with sad regret and a faint contempt for his passivity. Simon achieved a cholesterol level that would make people twenty years younger than he feel satisfied; his blood pressure was better than normal for his age. He was not overweight. He grew enamoured of the fact that he had played a major part in ensuring that his late middle-age was not blighted with illness. There is no greater solace, he believed increasingly, than taking control of one's own life. Let others dream of Elysium: for him the most potent myth was the one in which the little boy put his finger in the dyke, stemming the flow.

But his satisfaction was itself short-lived. Simon found that he began to be oppressed from another direction. Having conquered indolence through regular exercise and appetite through a strict diet, he found that he was left with the unbearably threatening fact that he lived in the most dangerous city in the world. He dreaded reading the newspaper and yet he read every page of it, morbidly. Not a day seemed to go by without someone – usually an elderly person who lived alone, as he did – being murdered in his or her home. Every day people were hijacked. The lucky ones survived, the others were killed. Johannesburg seemed to Simon to have become a place of siege, where the have-nots lay in wait and the haves lay in fear. It oppressed him more and more. As he took his vitamin supplements, his garlic-and-celery pills, his fish-oil tablets, as he continued to ensure that he drank one glass of red wine every night, all he could think was that in statistical terms he was more likely to be murdered, living in

Johannesburg, than any person living in any other place. That made him tense; then he considered that tension affects one adversely so he grew tense about being tense; that made him think that Johannesburg was killing him through fear, if not through crime. The teeth were snapping shut. What to do? What to do?

After a short period of morose self-pity and helpless anger, he became vigorously active on his own behalf. He sold his fashionable and expensive motor car and bought a modest second-hand car that suited him very well. Modest second-hand cars, he determined, are also in danger, but they are statistically less likely to be hijacked. Simon decided to put statistics on his side, rather than against him. Then he set out to make his house more secure. He already had bars on the windows, but they were not very sturdy; also, they were on the outside of the windows. He had them replaced with much thicker ones on the inside of the windows, which were cemented into the window sills. The rationale for this, according to the expert advice that he sought, is that it is extremely difficult to saw through bars or lever them away from the wall through broken glass, which is what the would-be burglars or assailants would have to do. It was very expensive, but Simon did not hesitate in having it done – it was an investment in his future. Then he had a wrought-iron door built in the passage which separated his bedroom from the rest of the house. This door had a special key which could not be replicated. He locked this door at night. This meant that, if intruders got into his house, they would not be able to get to him in the bedroom.

This was not all. The next thing was to have a sophisticated alarm system installed. There were panic buttons in every room in the house and scanners with red eyes that winked at him conspiratorially whenever he moved. He felt that he was being watched by his own house, which was a strange feeling; but soon he grew accustomed to it and considered that he had transformed his comfortable domestic environment into a sentry, standing guard on his behalf. It was not enough, in these straitened times, for his environment to offer him comfort only. It had to be vigilant too.

Then he bought a gun. This was a difficult decision and he agonized over it for a long time. What put him off was not so much the thought of having to use it or even of having to kill someone; rather it was the statistics which showed that people who owned a gun were in danger of being killed by that same gun, either through having it go off accidentally, or through having it used against them by someone else. But eventually he was persuaded by the argument that the mishaps occurred only when gun owners used them carelessly or injudiciously or ineffectively; so he determined that he would be guilty of none of these. He went for lessons and learned how to shoot. He turned out to be good at it, which was both surprising and encouraging. Then, having taken expert advice as to what would suit him best, he bought the gun. He kept it near him and treated it with reverential care, seeing himself more as its custodian than as its owner. The distinction was a fine one, but Simon upheld it for it might save his life.

Other precautions were available to him. He went out at night less and less; then he almost never went out after dark. He accepted lunch invitations, but never dinner invitations. He decided that he would not go to the centre of town unless it were really necessary. Then he realised that it never was really necessary, so he did not go there at all. He began to avoid areas that he considered unsafe. His old friend Leon lived in one such area, so he tried to get Leon to come to him every time they met. When Leon tired of the lack of reciprocity in these arrangements, Simon stopped seeing him altogether. He accepted sadly that Leon's disappointment and the fading of the long-standing friendship were the price of self-preservation. When Leon was mugged outside his flat a few weeks later, Simon felt sorry for him, yet somehow vindicated.

He found that he needed to leave his home less and less. He cancelled his subscription at the gym and bought several pieces of gym equipment instead, including an exercise bicycle. He found that some of the better stores would deliver food and groceries, so he opened accounts and bought exclusively from them. He knew that he was becoming a recluse, but who is not a recluse during a siege? He knew also that his wealth was protecting him from harm. Indeed, he could think of no better use for it. If his money was what people were after, then his money had better do something to protect itself. He had not been passive when it came to his health: he was certainly not going to be passive when he needed to defend himself. Over and over he told himself that he lived in the Murder Capital of the World. Murder Capital. Murder Capital. These were words of fearful fascination, like Beelzebub or Mephistopheles.

After the gun came an electrified fence around the property, as well as a Rottweiler called Nemesis. Then Simon was invited to a meeting of the residents of his suburb. Because it was called to address the problem of soaring crime in that area, he went. At the meeting, an accountant (who lived four houses away) and a restaurant-owner (who lived in the next street) proposed a drastic scheme to respond to the drastic situation. Simon was astounded to hear what they were proposing: he had not considered for a moment that such a thing could be feasible. The suggestion was that they seal off the suburb and restrict it to residents. Simon liked the idea from the start, but he felt convinced that it would, regrettably, either be impractical or legally impossible. The accountant and the restaurant-owner assured the people at the meeting that it was neither. The suburb was small; it had no main thoroughfares running through it; it was possible to limit access to it through three points of entry, each of which could be manned by armed guards. Anyone who was not a resident would have to sign in under the supervision of these guards, who would record the person's name, number-plate and the make and colour of the vehicle. Another suburb had recently been granted permission by the municipal authorities to fence itself in in this way. That suburb had already recorded a dramatic fall in crime.

After the first meeting, where people were asked to think it over, another meeting was held at the restaurant-owner's house. Although the meeting was at night, Simon broke his rule and went. An armed guard was employed to look after the residents' cars while the meeting was in progress. Simon believed that, if it were feasible, everyone would support the initiative. He found that he was wrong. The residents of the suburb differed considerably in their responses. The accountant and the restaurant-owner had the support of an orthopaedic surgeon, a retired insurance broker and two optometrists. But they found vehement opposition in an oncologist, a clinical psychologist, a physiotherapist, another accountant and two dentists. Simon did not speak up on behalf of the plan, but he turned repeatedly to the couple who were seated next to him and said, 'What else can we do? Something has got to be done. What else can we do?' Afterwards he found that they were amongst the opponents of the scheme. The accountant and the restaurant-owner asked the meeting for a mandate to investigate the practical and legal situation. They undertook to speak to the committee from the suburb that was already successfully enclosed and to establish the best course of action. A vote was taken and the mandate was granted by a narrow margin.

At the next meeting, the situation was more acrimonious and the two sides more entrenched in their positions. The oncologist made a speech which he had clearly thought about for a long time. He said that the moral implications bothered him more than the legal ones. Officialdom might grant them permission, but that didn't mean that they ought to proceed. He argued that the roads in the suburb were public property; they should not treat them as their own private property. Nor should they use the power of their affluence – he should say their relative affluence – to cut themselves off from the rest of the country, especially since it was the New South Africa, where barriers were supposed to be coming down. He understood people's anxieties; indeed, he shared them. But he could not condone a response that was the result of panic and hysteria. The clinical psychologist said that she would not live in such a suburb; she would sell her house. Simon was not persuaded at all by what they said, for the restaurant-owner kept repeating bluntly that 'what this was about was saving lives', and Simon found that to be the most eloquent argument of all. At that meeting the anti-enclosure side narrowly won the vote, much to his surprise. Their arguments seemed to him to be full of delicate qualms and he could see no place for such delicacy in an emergency. The accountant and the restaurant-owner, who had gathered a great deal of information, vowed that the matter would not end there.

Simon berated himself for not volunteering to do something as well; after all, he had the time. But he had never been that sort of person. He would sign petitions if he needed to and he would pay for the wall to be built around the suburb and for the guards' salaries, but he was prepared to leave it to others to make the arrangements.

For months he had read letters to the newspapers in which people lamented the descent of Johannesburg into a state of anarchy, describing (invariably) how they had greeted the advent of the New South Africa with euphoria and now they were bitter and fearful and thinking of emigrating. He admired these letter-writers and applauded their efforts, but he never wrote a letter himself. If a feeling prevails, it will find expression. Others more capable and articulate than he would give vent to this widespread disquiet.

Then, when people began to write letters to their local newspaper about the great dispute in his own suburb, Sterling Park, he felt suddenly that it was simply not good enough to remain passive. He had not been passive in the face of his unenviable genetic inheritance, nor had he done nothing when the security situation worsened. Now he should use that determination on behalf of his beleaguered suburb. His resolve was strengthened by an incident two streets away in which a man, returning from work, was hijacked in his driveway and shot twice. He was in hospital in a critical condition. The local newspaper that week reported this incident of violence prominently and included statistics which showed that the situation in the suburb was worsening; but it also carried a letter by the oncologist, arguing against the proposal to enclose the suburb. In it, he made the same points that he had used to persuade the meeting. He concluded by referring more explicitly to the affluence of the suburb. Money, he said, cannot buy everything – at least, it shouldn't be allowed to. Money should be held responsible for its excesses.

Something in this letter stirred Simon. He decided to write back. It would be the first time he had ever written a letter to the press. The fact that it was a local newspaper with a relatively small distribution was somehow consoling. He also liked the idea that he was writing to his own community about something that affected them as well as himself. He felt unusually public-spirited.

> *Sir,*
>
> *The letter by Dr Jenkins, published in your Letters Page on 24 March, requires a response. Dr Jenkins is hopelessly out of touch with public opinion. He is concerned about the rights of the public, but what about the rights of those who are killed or assaulted or robbed daily? This does not bother him unduly. Dr Jenkins forgets that we live in the Murder Capital of the World. We have to find ways of dealing with this emergency. Building a wall around Sterling Park is a sound and practical idea. We should give it our full support. Surely anything is better than being killed for our possessions, or becoming the victim of an act of irrational hatred?*

Simon thought of signing it 'Concerned Resident', but, in the spirit of his new activism and social commitment, he signed his name and included his address. He felt vaguely that his letter would not be published – no doubt, many of the residents would write in to take issue with the oncologist, and their letters would probably be far more forceful and persuasive than his. But, to his surprise, it was published the following week. He read it over several times and felt quite proud of it. Except for the fact that 'unduly' appeared as 'unduely', which bothered him because he would not like people to think that he couldn't spell correctly, he saw nothing in it that he felt was unworthy. It was short, to the point, and soundly logical.

The following week he was flattered to find that a number of people had written in response to his letter. People had read it and thought about it and several had considered it important enough to react. One person, identified only as 'Worried About Crime', wrote that Simon's letter, in focusing as it did on the very real peril that they faced on a daily basis, showed that Dr Jenkins and those who supported him were satisfying their own ideas of morality and conscience at the cost of other people's lives. A woman whom Simon had never heard of also wrote in support of his letter. After stating briefly that she agreed with him, she went on to recount at some length her experience of being hijacked one morning on her way to work.

The third letter took issue with Simon's. It was written by the husband of the clinical psychologist who had sided with the oncologist at the last meeting. He described himself as a retired architect who had lived in the suburb for over thirty years. The proposed enclosure of the suburb would not be dealing with crime, he said, it would be driving it elsewhere. Crime in the townships was far worse than in the largely white suburbs; this was a fact which was being overlooked. The proposal was the result of narrow self-interest and fear. South Africa had only recently come out of the laager, he wrote; he had no intention of allowing anyone to drive him back into it.

Simon thought of replying to the letter, but he decided that he had done his bit. The next edition of the newspaper produced a spate of letters on the subject, including one that referred both to his and the retired architect's: the letter-writer said that he would rather act out of fear than be dead and he thought that trying to save one's life and the lives of one's family was a legitimate form of self-interest, however narrow the retired architect thought this priority was. Simon approved of this letter. He felt gratified that his own letter could have helped to provoke such a fiery debate. He had begun to keep a file of all the articles and letters relating to the controversy and he added the latest batch, noting with pleasure that the number of letters in favour of the proposal far outweighed the number of dissenting responses. On the basis of this, public opinion was behind them.

A meeting of the supporters of the proposal was held at the accountant's home to consider strategy. People congratulated Simon on his letter and this time he did stand up to speak, emboldened by the success of the letter-writing. He said that he thought they should canvass opinion in the suburb to ascertain the attitudes of those residents who didn't come to meetings: they needed to know whether or not the majority of the residents of Sterling Park was behind them. He added that he felt certain that they were. People supported his suggestion and it was decided that a questionnaire would be distributed to every resident. Simon felt pleased with himself. There was something intoxicating about being part of a swelling consensus, he discovered; he regretted that he had not involved himself in community activities before this. The meeting ended with one man offering to draw up and photocopy the questionnaire, another offering to put one in every resident's post box, and Simon found himself volunteering to collate all the results once the questionnaires were in. Consequently, it was decided that residents would be asked to place completed questionnaires in Simon's post box. Then someone proposed that a name – something catchy – should be found for those who were working to bring the proposal to fruition. Several possibilities were thought of, but they finally settled on CLASP (Campaign to Limit Access to Sterling Park). Simon went home feeling proud, a little amused and somewhat surprised: he had been elected onto the organising committee of CLASP.

After that, things moved quickly. The questionnaires were drawn up and distributed and posters urging people to support CLASP and save lives appeared on tree trunks and lamp posts. The completed questionnaires began to trickle in. Simon became more interested in the contents of his post box than he had been for years. At first almost all the respondents were in favour of the proposal, but after a while an increasing number against it came in. Simon calculated the total every evening, and although those favourably disposed were still ahead, he noted that their lead was narrowing. What alarmed him was a note that he found one day amongst the questionnaires, addressed to him (although his name was wrongly spelt). It said, *Stop what you doing we will kill you*. A few days later there was another one saying, *If you do this you die*. Simon didn't know what to make of them – were they a joke? He showed them to the restaurant-owner, who told him breezily to ignore them. He tried to heed this advice, but he found that he couldn't. He became anxious about what he would find in his letterbox and the pleasant curiosity that he had begun to enjoy dissipated.

One day he went out briefly and returned to find a message on his answering machine. A thick and muffled voice, scarcely distinguishable, said 'You die soon, you die. You must stop what you doing.' Simon went to the police with the notes and the recorded message. They were so uninterested in his story that he had to urge them even to take down the details. The less concerned other people were, the more his anxiety grew. He began to sleep badly. When he did manage to fall asleep, Nemesis would begin to bark and he would awake with a jolt. He got up repeatedly during the night to make sure that he had set the alarm before he went to bed. He kept opening the drawer next to his bed to check that the gun was close at hand.

The questionnaires continued to trickle in. Simon watched the lead that CLASP had established at the beginning grow smaller and smaller. For a while the two sides were equal, then the votes against enclosing the suburb drew ahead. Every day the situation grew worse. Nonetheless, he continued to believe that it would turn in their favour again. He could not accept that there were more people who sympathised with the views of the oncologist and the clinical psychologist and the retired architect than those who felt that staying alive was the most important thing in life. How could so basic and primal a need not overrule all else? Eventually the questionnaires stopped coming in and Simon had to present the final tally. CLASP had lost by nineteen votes. After imparting the news, he awaited what he believed to be the inevitable response: a renewed campaign, more letters, door-to-door discussions with those who had voted against it to persuade them to change their minds. He was prepared to participate fully in all of these efforts. He was astonished to find that nothing of the sort was proposed. The members of CLASP accepted their defeat with dismaying resignation. Even the accountant and the restaurant-owner gave in. The accountant said he would sell his house and move – either to the suburb that had enclosed itself, or into a town-house complex where there were armed guards and surveillance twenty-four hours a day. The restaurant-owner said his wife had been urging him for months to emigrate; he thought after this that perhaps she was right.

Simon went home full of flat, chilly sadness. He wished that he had never had anything to do with CLASP at all. To see all his enthusiasm and energy come to nothing was devastating. He felt bitter and angry. If people were attacked or murdered in Sterling Park after this, they would have no one but themselves to blame. But what if the victim were someone like him, someone who had fought for the plan? Then it would be his unreasonable, impervious neighbours, full of moral niceties, who would be to blame. The very community that he had sought to protect would then be an accomplice in the crime.

There was another message on the machine. The same indistinct voice said 'We coming for you. You must die soon.' Simon unplugged the phone and the answering-machine. He went to the corner cafe, which stayed open till late at night, and bought what he had ignored for years: chocolates, salty potato crisps, marshmallows, ice cream and biltong. The biltong didn't look very good – it was greyish and gnarled, but he bought it anyway. At home, instead of doing his exercises, he sat in front of the television and began to eat what he had bought. Hours went by. There was nothing good on the television, but he watched it anyway. Then a late movie came on. It was Audrey Hepburn in *Wait Until Dark*. For years Simon had refused to watch thrillers, as a matter of principle. But he watched this one, without the lights on. The television cast rushing shapes and shadows on the wall behind him.

Crowd Control

Harold hated the middle of summer – not for what it was, but for what it brought. As the month of December approached, he would begin to brace himself for six or seven weeks of torment. He knew that the holiday crowds benefited the city economically; he knew that every restaurant-owner, every proprietor of a guest-house, everyone who had a stall at a flea market must welcome the pleasure-seekers and their money. At a level within himself where there was pragmatism and common sense – a sort of mezzanine level, full of light and plastic plants – Harold could accept that, as a resident of Cape Town, there should be some kind of welcome within him too.

But at another level, deep in the basement of his heart, Harold felt all the anxieties of one entering a torture chamber. For those weeks of high summer there would be no hope of tranquillity within him, no space in his fretful unease for himself, just as there was virtually no space for him on the street, on the pavement, on the promenade in Sea Point, where he liked to walk in the afternoon, or in the restaurant where he liked to eat twice a week. Soon they would be here, those for whom pleasure was a ruthless ambition, greedy for sun and fun, pushing at him and past him with all the terrible chauvinism of young flesh.

He would not leave the city during those months, even though there was no practical reason why he should not do so, for he was retired and could afford to take a holiday in a less popular part of the world. But he would not, for that would be like surrendering to the marauders. And so there was nothing for him to do but to retreat within his resentment; and to wait; and to hate. He indulged to the full his hatred of the crowds – of their shoving, their shouting, their hooting, their demanding anonymity. And why should he not hate, after all, seeing as he never did anything with his hatred? To hate and not to harm: what could possibly be wrong with that? And the hatred of those who were anonymous was such a vague, diffused kind of hatred, for all its keenness; it could not reach them in the least.

Once he was in his flat, he could block out the sight of the crowds, although he could not avoid entirely the sound of them. From the street below, he could hear the heedless noises that they made as they annexed for their pleasure even that time which has been called the small hours of the morning, but which, in their hands, was now grown large and brash. Harold could see the sea from his flat: the setting sun was a presence in his sitting-room. He would watch, a respectful onlooker, as it performed its quiet and solitary ablutions in the Atlantic every afternoon. But now the ritual brought him no pleasure, for that same sun had spent the day pleasing the crowds on the beaches, pandering to them like a courtesan; and now, tainted with their satisfaction, it sank into the sea, leaving the hot, fuzzy night to indulge them in its absence.

At the level within himself where he could be sternly rational, Harold knew that he was over-reacting, yet he seemed unable to stop himself. It was the same as his morbid anxieties about the population explosion. Ever since he was a child, Harold had been terrified of the population explosion. He used to lie awake at night, torturing himself with scenarios of ghastly claustrophobia. The earth had become a catacomb into which the living hordes were thrust. He would have to share a room with eleven others. He would have to live in a broom cupboard. He would have to be put down when he reached forty years of age because there was no more air or food for him. No one cared who or what he was, only that he breathed and ate, and that was unforgivable.

When he spoke soberly to himself, he knew that there was nothing to fear. The population explosion was a receding threat. Affluent countries had falling birth rates; in some cases, deaths exceeded births. The solution was obvious: improve the conditions of people's lives and the babies would stop coming. And if the world could not heed the simple lesson, what was it to him? He would be dead long before the situation could ever begin to affect him.

But in the murkier regions where his fear lay, the possibility of the world's controlling its spawning meant nothing. Harold thought of places he had never been to, never would visit: Bangladesh, for instance; or Ethiopia. When he lay awake at night, he would think of Bangladesh and Ethiopia. He didn't know what to do about them. He saw dirty furrows and water thick as pus. Wailing babies appeared, born out of the yellow water itself, born with pot bellies and wizened faces, wave upon wave of them, murderous, dying babies. And he hated them so. He hated their rapaciousness and their terrible feebleness that nothing could oppose. And he hated Mother Teresa, who nursed them instead of giving them condoms. And he wondered where one could hide from these malnutrants. There is not enough to go around, he thought: if some have, others must do without. He would not give what he had to them, for they were insatiable and their need was like a void: they would not even notice that anything had been given to them, while he would be left with nothing.

To try to calm himself down, he would think of uninhabited places: of a vast savannah where the horizon was further away than it had ever been, so far that even the clouds could not reach it. No human figure appeared here to disturb the wave-like motion of the grass. This was the unpopulated world that came before – the clean world; or perhaps it was the depopulated world that comes after – the cleansed world. He longed for that world, even if it meant that he could not be a part of it. And he felt vaguely that he was not alone in wishing for it; that there must have been others, especially in this crowded century, who had longed for it too. He did not know who they were, yet he felt a vague sense of kinship with these people.

He spent as much time as he could in his flat, waiting for the acute period of high summer to pass. When he was forced to go out, he tried always to lessen the ordeal of the crowded streets by spending time in the Sea Point library. He found the muffled noises and the discreet librarians soothing. The only drawback to the library was that he was inclined to meet Bennie there. He had known the man for thirty years. The fact that they had nothing at all in common was known only to him; Bennie had remained quite unaware of this fact for three decades. Invariably Bennie spoke too loudly, greeted too effusively, said too much – about his wife, his five children, his eighteen grandchildren. He recommended books that held no interest for Harold: after all these years, Bennie had still not realised how far apart their sensibilities lay. When he was there, Harold would choose his books hurriedly; otherwise, he would spend hours in the library, browsing contentedly, almost forgetting the horrors that awaited him as soon as he stepped outside.

Last summer he had found another haven – an antique shop which he came across one day in a quiet side-street. It was called *Exclusive Cape Antiques*. Inside the shop it was cool and dark. A ceiling fan sifted the air unobtrusively, while a grandfather clock, refusing to be hurried, admonished the cowed hours. He began to look forward to his visits. He felt reassured by the sedateness of the shop, by its unruffled air. It was a reticent place; that was what he liked best. More often than not, he bought nothing. Even if no new artefacts had come in since he was last there, he didn't care. He was happy to look again at what he had already admired.

The proprietor, an elderly woman, surveyed all with a stately air. One or two customers would come in – discerning people who knew what they wanted, knew far more about antiques than Harold did, if the truth be told, but what did it matter? He was beginning to learn. As his confidence grew, he bought something every now and then, but always something small, for there was no room in his flat for anything large. Although he loved the old wooden furniture – some of it more than two hundred years old: the country cupboards made of kiaat or cedarwood, the half-moon tables made of stinkwood with yellowwood inlay, the stinkwood display cabinets – he would have had nowhere to put any of them. There was no point cluttering his flat. But a silver snuff box or sauce ladle, a crystal decanter, six sherry glasses – these things would not rob him of his space. He bought them slowly, savouring the pleasure of the acquisition.

The elderly proprietor, as she grew accustomed to seeing him in the shop, became friendlier and, eventually, quite chatty. She told him that she and her husband started the shop more than forty years ago, when they came out from Europe. She extended a beringed hand. 'I am Mrs Frank,' she said. Harold shook her hand. He was gratified to find her becoming less stern. Mrs Frank seemed to him to be like one of those severe headmistresses whose crusty exterior hides a rough kindness; the sort of person of whom people always say afterwards that her bark was worse than her bite.

What pleased him too was that, after this, she took a greater interest in his purchases, telling him that what he had bought was rare; it was unusual; very few were ever made; very few still existed. As he fought his way home through the crowds that moved as if with one mind to the video stores, the hamburger stands, the ice cream vendors, leaving polystyrene cups strewn behind them, he felt grateful that there was still such precious singularity in the world.

Some of Mrs Frank's clients had been buying from her for decades, she told him: she had very loyal customers, very loyal. Harold felt that their loyalty was being offered to him, so that he could partake of it too. He was being invited to begin his own long relationship with *Exclusive Cape Antiques*. 'Anything you want, you tell me,' said the old woman. 'I get it for you. You just tell me.' There was nothing that Harold wanted in particular, but her assumption that he was a serious collector of antiques flattered him; so, after much thought, he told her that he wanted a gold fob-chain. 'No problem,' she replied, 'I can get it for you.' And within three weeks he had it.

It was like being admitted to an elite club. What was needed in order to become a member was the ability to appreciate what the shop had to offer, to see that there had been occasions in the past when prescient individuals had stood back from the remorseless welter of the world, and that what was sold in the shop was the stuff of that momentous pause. Let the lemmings run, Harold thought; let them run past me and leave me behind.

Mrs Frank began increasingly to confide in Harold. He felt honoured, as if the privilege of her conversation were in itself one of the precious items on offer in the shop. He learned that she had managed the shop alone for eight years and presumed that this was because her husband was dead. She told him, however, that her husband was still alive, although gravely ill with emphysema. He lay at home, tended by a full-time nurse, unable to do without his oxygen canisters. After that, Harold felt obliged to enquire after her husband every time he came into the shop. She would sigh and shake her head. 'He is not good. How can he be good?' she would say; but he could see that she was pleased by the enquiry.

'Do you have any children?' he asked her once after the routine enquiry about her husband. 'Will there be anyone to see to the shop when you are gone?'

'We have no children,' she said. 'And what about you? Do you have any?'

'No.'

'Then we are the same. We are the last of our breed.'

'Well, at least we have not added to the population explosion,' Harold said, smiling.

'No, that is not us,' she said. 'We do not do that. We never have. It is them.' She indicated the street outside. 'It is them. The Africans. They have babies like rabbits. Like flies. It is a big problem.'

Something struck Harold about the shop one day, something that, oddly, he had not noticed on all his previous visits. He waited until Mrs Frank had finished dealing with a customer, so that he could ask her about it. 'Tell me,' he said, 'why do you stock South African antiques? Why not European antiques? I would have thought, in view of your background ...'

'No,' she said, before he had finished the sentence. 'No, my husband

and I were not interested in that. Europe is finished. Finished. South Africa is our home. It has been good to us. Although we deal with old things, we cannot live in the past.'

Harold found these sentiments surprising. He had thought of Mrs Frank as a sort of displaced European aristocrat, a remnant of a stately, pre-War Europe that was now gone. He had taken for granted in her a nostalgia, a measure of scorn for the newness of South Africa. But this was not the case. 'There is history here too,' she said. 'Look at the beautiful things in this shop. They show us that the past is here also. South Africa is a young country, but it is an old country too. We have never felt that we did not have a place here or that we do not belong. We are happy to die here.'

'I'm pleased to hear it,' said Harold. He thought about what she had said for some time. That night he held the fob-chain in his hand and thought: this is what has been salvaged. This is the precious thing that lies amidst the dross. It is here, if only I can keep finding it and never lose sight of it. That is what she is trying to tell me.

When he went to the shop a few days later, he could scarcely believe what he saw. All the shop windows were broken, the pavements were covered in glass and policemen were sifting through the debris. Mrs Frank stood in the street, agitated and breathless, her usual composure wholly abandoned. 'Look at this!' she shouted, as soon as she saw Harold. 'Look! Look what they have done!'

'Who?' he asked. 'Who has done this?'

'They go past,' she said. 'They are singing and making a noise. Then they smash the windows, they take things from the shop, some of them they smash, they just throw them down in the street.'

'Who?' he asked. 'Who?'

But Mrs Frank ignored his question. She told someone else how the windows had been broken, how the precious goods had been vandalised. 'This is what will destroy this country,' she said, waving her arms wildly. 'No one can control them. They move in groups like animals and then they become like animals.'

Harold eventually managed to establish what had happened. A group of striking workers had gone past the shop, chanting slogans and singing. No one seemed to know who they were: someone said they were refuse collectors, but someone else insisted that it was the postal workers who were on strike. There was even the unlikely suggestion that they were all messengers-of-court. They turned off the main street, using the side-street as a short cut to the foreshore; and then, suddenly, no one seemed to know why, they had attacked Mrs Frank's shop. In five minutes the damage was done and they moved off.

'Never have we had any problems,' Mrs Frank was telling the people who gathered in the street to look at the devastation. 'In forty years we have had no problems. We make no trouble, we have no trouble. Now it starts. These things that they have broken, they cannot be replaced. Never. They are one of a kind. Now it starts. This is the beginning, but I can see the end. Better that we die now, my husband and me.'

She protested that she did not want to leave the shop, but, eventually, someone persuaded her to get into a car and she was driven away. The shards of glass on the pavement were being swept up. Harold felt that there was no longer any point in staying there. In the rather hysterical response of Mrs Frank there was, he felt, some truth. It did feel like the beginning of the end, but he could not say of what.

He went to the library, needing to feel that one of his havens was still available to him. He prayed that Bennie would not be there, but, of course, there he was, beaming broadly and pressing a book on him.

He tried to resist, but Bennie was persistent and Harold, still shaken by what he had seen at the shop, felt that it was easier to give in than stand and argue. He scarcely listened to what Bennie was saying about it. As he made his escape, however, he heard him say, 'You'll find it fascinating – even you, a lapsed Jew.'

'I'm not a lapsed Jew,' he said. 'I'm a non-religious Jew.'

'I'm joking,' Bennie shouted from across the street. 'Can't you take a joke?'

That night Harold struggled to get to sleep. When he did sleep, he was afflicted by nightmares. In one of them the babies from Bangladesh and Ethiopia appeared, but this time they were here, in Cape Town. They were as scrawny as ever, but for once they were not simply lying around, weak and dying. They ran, quick as monkeys. He followed them down the streets, knowing, with a morbid certainty, that they were heading for *Exclusive Cape Antiques*. Sure enough, they swarmed into the shop and he followed them in, unable to break away. They paid him no attention, yet they held him in thrall. He could hear their screeches of delight as they held the trinkets up to the light, before they dropped and smashed everything. They climbed onto the furniture and excreted all over it. He wondered how they managed to produce excrement in such vast quantities, seeing as they had not eaten anything since they were born. He felt he had to find Mrs Frank, to protect her from them, but he could not see her anywhere. He grew more frantic and then he awoke.

It was four in the morning and there was no chance now of falling asleep again. There was drunken shouting coming up from the street below. He went to get something to drink. On his way back from the kitchen, he saw the books he had brought from the library on the dining-room table. He looked at them again and then, idly, he picked up the one that Bennie had urged him to take and began to glance through it. To his surprise, he didn't find it boring at all. It was a book written by a Jewish doctor from Johannesburg. The doctor was an amateur historian. He had become interested in what had happened to the Nazis and Nazi collaborators who fled Europe at the end of the War. Whereas it was widely known that a large number of them had made their way to South America, the doctor sought to show in his book that it was less well known, but nonetheless the case, that a substantial number had come to southern Africa too: to South West Africa in particular, but also to South Africa. The doctor had done a great deal of careful research and Harold found the argument credible. He became engrossed in the book.

What the doctor's discoveries meant was that these people had been living hidden amongst them all the time. They had slipped undetected into the general population and were protected by the mass of humankind which, despite its reputation, is a great deal less curious than one would think. No one had paused to single them out, but this is what the doctor now did. At the back of the book he included in an appendix what was, perhaps, the most interesting part of his enquiry – certainly, it was the most tangible. He listed alphabetically the names of those individuals whom he had managed to identify, specifying what they had done during the War and adding whatever information he had regarding what had happened to them since they came to southern Africa. Many of them, of course, were dead. A surprisingly large percentage, however, were still alive. Harold ran his eye down the list. The words 'living at present in Cape Town' caught his attention and he paused to read the entry. The man's name was Wilhelm Franz. He was one of those who, from the autumn of 1941 onwards, supervised the deportation of German Jews from metropolitan Germany to Polish and Soviet ghettoes in the east. These Jews were crowded into goods or cattle wagons and many did not survive the journey. Wilhelm Franz, Harold read, had been the proprietor for over forty years of an antique shop called *Exclusive Cape Antiques*.

He put the book down on the table and walked to the window. The street below was quite still now; even the late-night revellers had fallen silent at last. The sun had not yet risen, although there was a tell-tale pinkness in the east. The sky and the sea had the world to themselves.

The Wheels of God

The town in which Ina lived was uninspiringly new. Sue could only think of it as an instant town, created yesterday, even though it was probably nearly twenty years old. It had been determined during the years of South Africa's isolation that it was necessary to convert more coal into fuel and a large town had come into existence as a result: a whole town, summoned with a click of the fingers out of the empty veld, as meek as if the mandarins of the old Nationalist government had been as omnipotent as God. And here it stood, all its history as new as a scab that has not yet been shed.

Sue thought she would remember where Ina's house was, but it was too long since her last visit and her vague memories proved to be inadequate. After a while, she accepted that she was lost. A petrol-attendant set her in the right direction, and then she found it quite easily. She looked at the houses that lined the quiet Sunday-morning streets, wondering what it must be like to live in them and why it was that the inhabitants did not get out while they still could. These soporific houses must have a secret power, some sort of drug which they administered to the people who lived in them so that they remained docile and compliant. 'There but for the grace of God go I,' thought Sue.

That was one of the sayings she had kept with her from her childhood, from her mother's stock of truisms. Her mother was a great believer in received wisdom: she found it in these aphoristic hand-me-downs. She offered them solemnly as if uncorking bottles of vintage wine. Sue, on the other hand, had misgivings about most of them and never sought them out deliberately, but they flitted nonetheless into her mind from time to time. Because she could not prevent them from coming, she made them mean what she wanted them to mean. In this case, for instance, she didn't believe in grace or in God, but she was prepared to use the saying when she wanted to remind herself of a lucky escape. Looking about her at this town, she considered that, whatever misfortunes she had met with in life, this crushing blandness, this jaded newness, she had at least escaped. In fact, until she met Glenda, it had not even come her way. But Glenda and her mother, Ina, had lived in a succession of platteland towns, each, Glenda had said, worse than the previous one. This town, to which Ina had moved after Glenda had already left home, was undoubtedly the worst. The few times Sue and Glenda had come there together to visit Ina, towards the beginning of their relationship, Glenda had grown quiet and distant, as if seeing in the town the declension of her mother's life and of her own childhood.

Sello was growing restless. He hated long car journeys. 'We're nearly there,' Sue said to him. 'Just wait a few more moments.' She found Ina's house and parked in the street, but Ina appeared at the front door, calling to her to pull the car into the driveway. Ina kissed her on the cheek and then didn't seem to know how to respond to Sello. He, in turn, became shy and clung to Sue. 'Here's Ina,' she said to him. 'Granny Ina. Do you remember her?' There was no way he could, of course. He had probably only seen her twice in his life and he had certainly not seen her since Glenda's death. He shook his head and was silent. 'He's shy,' she said apologetically.

'Come inside,' said Ina. 'I'm sure you want something to drink.'

They followed her inside, Sue carrying her overnight bag into which she had managed to squeeze a change of clothes for herself and Sello for the next day as well as some of his books and toys. The house inside was dark, very clean and austere. There was a framed copy of the *Desiderata* on the wall in the sitting-room. Because it was there, phrases from it came unbidden to Sue, like a monotonous tune that one cannot get out of one's head: *Avoid loud and aggressive persons ... The universe is unfolding as it should*. She thought it might be possible to sing *the universe is unfolding as it should* to the tune of *London Bridge is Falling Down*. Another possibility was *Here We Go Round the Mulberry Bush*: *the universe is unfolding as it should, as it should ...*

Enough! She rebuked herself, but not sternly, and paid attention instead to what Ina was saying. 'I wasn't sure where to put him,' said Ina. 'Will he sleep in a room on his own?'

'No,' said Sue. 'Put him in with me.'

She left the overnight bag in the bedroom that she and Sello would share and then they all sat down at the kitchen table. Sue and Ina drank tea, while Sello had a glass of orange squash. Ina put a plate of biscuits in front of him. 'Choose the one you want and eat it,' Sue said to him. 'Don't touch them all.'

After a while, Ina said, 'Sue, I want to thank you for coming to see me.'

'Thank you for the invitation,' said Sue. 'We haven't seen you since the funeral.'

There was a silence. 'How have you been?' Sue asked.

'Not too bad. And you?'

'I have my days. And Sello can be difficult. He misses Glenda. Being a single parent was never one of my plans, I can tell you.' Ina made no reply. 'But I have no regrets,' Sue went on. 'He's a lovable little boy. Glenda adored him. I cannot look at him without thinking how much she loved him and how much happiness he gave her in the last years of her life.'

She considered her own words with mild astonishment. They seemed to have sidled out of her mouth while she wasn't looking. Without setting out to do so, she could see herself marking her territory, claiming the dead Glenda for herself and for Sello, rebuking Glenda's mother with the limits of her knowledge and influence, hinting – more than hinting – that her love had fallen short. The habit of fighting for Glenda was so strong that it seemed to have survived Glenda herself.

Ina said, 'Would you mind very much if I got straight to the point? I've invited some people for lunch and once they arrive, we won't be able to talk. I know it's not very polite to bombard you as soon as you walk in.'

'Please go ahead,' said Sue. 'I'm not offended in the least.'

'I haven't been very well lately,' said Ina. 'I suppose old age is creeping up on me. I'm sure I'll be around for quite a while, but, in any case, I decided recently that I must get my will sorted out. After Glenda died, I changed it in favour of my sister, who lives in Durban. But now I want to change it again.'

Sello was growing restless once more. Sue asked if they could take him outside to play in the back garden. 'He's been cooped up in the car for hours,' she said. 'You can't blame him.'

Sello scurried ahead of them. He was content to be left to play by himself. 'Call me if you want me,' Sue said to him.

'Okay,' he said.

'See ya later, alligator,' said Sue.

'In a while, crocodile,' answered Sello.

When they sat down again, Ina said, 'I've decided that I want to leave everything I have to this child. Also, I have a policy coming due this year which I want to make over to him now, while I'm still alive. I don't really need it for myself.'

'I see,' said Sue. Her mother would have said 'Miracles will never cease.' Sue didn't believe in miracles, so for her the expression merely signified astonishment. A number of comments came to mind, but they were all faintly sarcastic, so she said nothing.

'I've thought about it for a long time,' Ina said. 'This is what I want to do.'

'You didn't need to tell me of this decision,' said Sue. 'You could simply have changed your will in his favour and put the money from the policy away for him.'

'No, I wanted to discuss it with you. Firstly, I don't even know what his proper name is. I'm sorry.'

'His first names are Sello Michael. It's spelt S-e-l-l-o. Those are the names he had when Glenda and I adopted him. His surname, of course, is Glenda's. In other words, it's the same as yours.'

All her efforts notwithstanding, some sarcasm was creeping in. She told herself to be more careful.

'The other thing,' said Ina, 'is what exactly to do with the money. I'm not a wealthy woman, but this house is paid off. He would get quite a lot. Should I leave it in trust, with yourself as the trustee, so that it can be used one day for his education?'

'If you really want to do something for him,' said Sue, 'you should leave it to me to use on his behalf. And you should make the policy over to me as soon as the money becomes available. I'm sorry to be so blunt, but you wanted to know what I think. So I'm telling you.'

Ina hesitated.

'You don't have to worry,' said Sue. 'I won't use a cent of it for myself. It will all be for him.'

'I don't doubt that,' said Ina. 'I just want to do what's best. That's why I asked you to come here.'

'What is best is what I have told you.'

Sue went to check on Sello. She watched him through the window. There were no burglar bars on any of the windows. She always noticed these things; she supposed she always would. There had been no bars on the windows of the ground-floor flat in Johannesburg they were living in eight years ago – the flat which Sue had liked and which they had rented despite Glenda's reservations, because Glenda liked to indulge her. Someone had broken in and, finding Glenda there alone, had raped her and beaten her brutally, leaving her for dead. Not Glenda's courage, not her determination to recover her life, not the adoption of Sello four years later – nothing had made Sue feel that what that event had done to them both could ever be ameliorated. One could live around it, but one could never dislodge it. Sue wondered whether the town really was so safe and peaceful, or whether Ina ought to be more cautious and install burglar bars.

There was a framed photograph of Glenda in the bedroom, aged about eighteen. In other rooms there were photographs of her when she was a baby or still at school. Predictably, there were no photographs taken during the last ten years of her life, nothing from the period in which she and Sue were together, nothing from the years in which they lived together with Sello as a family. Ina had kept with her only the Glenda she approved of. It was as if the Glenda who had loved another woman and who had adopted a little black boy had been wiped out. Yet that woman and that little boy were all that she had left to her now. It was a cruel retribution, too cruel even for Ina. Sue had never forgiven her for choosing to see as little as possible of Glenda during the last years of her life, for her ostentatious coldness towards them all. She had thought at the time that there was no punishment severe enough for a woman who rejected her only child. Yet now she felt that there was no crime severe enough for this punishment.

More trespassing words crept up on her. *The wheels of God grind slowly* she thought. This was a corruption of another of her mother's maxims. Making her voice as stern and declamatory as possible, her mother used to say *the mills of God grind slowly, yet they grind exceeding small*. (It was strange to think how many of her sayings made reference to God, considering that her mother was not a particularly religious woman. God, it seemed, was indispensable when it came to aphorisms.) When she was a child, Sue thought her mother said *the wheels of God* instead of *the mills of God*. Even when she learned what it was supposed to be, she thought *the wheels of God* sounded better, so it stuck. She spent most of her childhood in awe of that saying, frightened of the wheels of God and the relentless monosyllables in which they seemed to thunder along; but she had had no idea of what it all meant. Later, when the meaning came to her one day, unmasking the familiar words as if bringing a spy in the house to light, she found the expression disappointingly banal. It all seemed to be about retribution and reward. Wait long enough, it seemed to say, and the retribution or the reward will come. Well, big deal.

Sello was calling her. 'Sue-Ma ... Sue-Ma.' (He had always called them 'Sue-Ma' and 'Glenda-Ma'.) She went out to the back yard. Sello had found out that if he lifted up the stones that lay scattered about the rockery, great discoveries were to be made. He showed her the scuttling creatures that lived beneath the stones, inviting her to share in his excitement. Glenda would have been able to tell him what they all were. Sue tried her best. She showed him that some of the ants were red and others were black. The long, slow, black millipede, she told him, was a shongololo. Sello repeated the word to himself: *shongololo*. He was at the age where he could appreciate the sheer deliciousness of words, and, Sue thought, smiling to herself, they don't get more delicious than shongololo. That was all she could tell him about the insects, but he seemed satisfied. 'We're going to have lunch,' she said. 'Let's go and wash.'

They went inside. Ina was setting the table. 'Can I help?' Sue asked.

'Thank you, but it's all done.'

Ina covered the table with a net. 'The flies are very bad here,' she said. Sue took Sello to the bathroom. When they came back, Ina said, 'Did Glenda ever mention a girl called Veronica Johnson? They were at school together in Brakpan.'

'Yes.' Veronica had been Glenda's first great friend. Afterwards Glenda realised that it was her first great love, but she didn't think in those terms at the time. She had recounted anecdotes of their friendship and Sue, who had been jealous, had pretended to find them amusing.

'You won't believe it, but she's living here now. She works in the library. Her husband is the town clerk. She's Veronica Schutte now. She recognised me immediately. Isn't life full of extraordinary coincidences?'

'Indeed.'

'I invited them for lunch today. They want to meet you.'

The guests arrived not long afterwards. Veronica and her husband, Pieter, resembled each other – they looked more like brother and sister than husband and wife. They were both tall and good-looking in a toothy sort of way. 'I was always sorry that Glenda and I lost touch,' said Veronica. 'When her Mom walked into the library one day, I couldn't believe my eyes. I was so excited. I thought: here is the chance to get together with Glenda again. Then she told me about the car accident. I was devastated.'

'Yes,' said Sue. 'The most careful driver in the world. The one who didn't drink at the office party so that she could drive the others home. And someone shoots through a red traffic light. Everyone else survives and Glenda is killed. And that's that.'

'So much for caution,' said Veronica.

She should only know, thought Sue. She should only know. The perverse ironies were far greater and far crueller than any Veronica imagined. She should only know that this was the same woman who had survived an attack which left her with a clot on the brain and a ruptured spleen. Never mind caution. So much for courage and resilience and insisting on the future. Sue's mother would have said *Man proposes, God disposes*.

'I'm so pleased to meet you,' said Veronica. 'And your little boy. Ina has spoken of you both.'

Then Pieter said, lowering his voice, 'Ina's a very special woman, is she not? So dignified, despite all her troubles.'

'Yes,' said Sue. Ina's dignity was not something she could appreciate, for it had been too much a part of her aloofness and intransigence, and therefore of that which had wounded Glenda. But she did not begrudge Ina the admiration of these people.

During lunch, Pieter and Veronica assured Sue that the town was not as arid a place as it seemed. There was a theatre in which plays, ballet, musicals and even an opera or two had been staged. There were a number of educated, professional people like themselves who, being newly qualified, had seen the mushroom town as a place of opportunity. 'It's not often nowadays that people can feel like pioneers,' said Pieter. Then there was some perfunctory talk of Gilbert and Sullivan, Gershwin and Prokofiev, Wilde and Shaw.

When Ina went to the kitchen to see to the dessert, Veronica said, 'Speaking of pioneers, I hope you won't feel that we're being too personal if we say that we admire you so. The adoption of this little boy is such a wonderful thing. I thought it was amazing when Ina told me about it, but now that I see you together, I realise even more how incredible it is.'

'It was Glenda's idea. I wasn't keen at first, but I came round to it eventually. The credit for it is Glenda's.'

'Did you not consider having a child of your own?' asked Pieter. 'You know, through insemination?'

'I hope you don't feel we're prying,' said Veronica. 'We feel so relaxed with you. It's like being with an old friend.'

'Not at all,' said Sue. 'Yes, we did think of that. But Glenda wanted to go for the adoption instead. She had quite specific reasons for wanting it that way.'

'And now you're bringing up a black child – all on your own! Are you going to cope?'

'I have no choice,' said Sue.

Ina came back into the room. She had baked an apple tart, which they ate with cream. Sello didn't want any and was given a bowl of ice cream instead. 'Thank you,' said Sue. 'He loves ice cream.'

Veronica, she noticed, made no attempt to speak of her friendship with Glenda when they were girls. Sue couldn't decide if she was relieved or disappointed. When the relationship with Glenda grew more secure, she had ceased to feel jealous of Glenda's past; but, now that Glenda was herself the past, she found herself feeling possessive and territorial once more.

Pieter was talking about the town again. 'There's a great deal of unemployment and hardship here amongst the white people,' he said. 'Job security's gone. Affirmative Action has reached even the platteland.'

'There was always Affirmative Action on the platteland,' said Sue. 'The only difference is that whites, especially Afrikaners, were the beneficiaries. What's happening now is merely the consequence of what was done before.' She felt irritated with herself as she spoke. Why was she getting into this? These kinds of conversations never achieved anything; no one's mind was ever changed. All they did was create ill-feeling.

'I suppose,' said Pieter, 'that what it boils down to is this: is the New South Africa about moving forward or is it about retribution? Progress or punishment? Which is it to be?'

'Forgive me,' said Sue. 'How ungenerous of me to harp on the past.'

To her surprise, Veronica leaned forward and squeezed her hand. 'It's all right,' she said, as if Sue had burst into tears. 'We understand.'

Sue fought to repress a violent inclination to laugh. She wondered why she had exercised so much restraint. There was a time when she would have been much more combative. If Glenda were still alive, she would have wanted to show Veronica up, to emphasise to Glenda how unworthy her first love was – or had become. She would have seized every opportunity to rub it in. For reasons that went beyond Glenda and their relationship – political reasons, for want of a better word – she would have let nothing pass. But now it didn't seem worth the effort. There was certainly nothing new in this town and she was tired of old struggles, especially insidious ones.

Sello suddenly lost his shyness and went through his repertoire of rhymes and songs. *Pop Goes the Weasel* appeared unexpectedly in the middle of songs from *The Lion King*.

'Amazing how they still learn the same things that we learned as children!' said Veronica.

'Not in my case,' said Sue. 'I wouldn't dream of teaching him some of the things I learned as a child.'

Veronica found a sucker in her hand-bag and gave it to Sello. When Pieter and Veronica left, they both hugged Sue and urged her to visit again soon. 'You could stay with us,' said Veronica. 'But I don't imagine that Ina would be prepared to give you up.'

'No, certainly not,' said Ina.

After they had gone, Ina and Sue washed the dishes together. 'Aren't they nice?' asked Ina. 'Such a delightful couple. Broad-minded, too.'

'Very nice.'

Then Ina said, 'I want to go back to the subject of the money. I still don't understand why you don't want me to put it in trust for Sello until he's older. You won't need large amounts of money when he's still small.'

'As I said before, you'll have to accept that I know what's best for him. That's my advice. Of course, the decision is yours and you will do whatever you prefer.'

Ina scrubbed at the bottom of a pot with a pot-scourer and then she said, 'Is this child sick?'

'No,' said Sue.

'Please tell me the truth. Is that why you think you may need the money? Is he sick?'

'No.'

'Sue, don't play games with me. I'm not as stupid as you think.'

'I've never considered you stupid.'

'Then answer me. Has this child got Aids?'

'No.'

'HIV?'

'Yes.' There was a long silence. They did not look at each other.

'When did you find out?'

'We always knew. He was like that when we adopted him.'

'You adopted him, knowing that he had it? That he will die?'

'I don't believe that he will die. But yes, we knew.'

'But why? Why?'

'It was Glenda's decision. She wanted to adopt a child, not have one herself. And she wanted it to be a boy. And she was prepared to take an HIV child. It's not easy to explain it to you. Glenda would have explained it better if you'd been around at the time. It had something to do with the fact that she survived the attack and that she didn't get HIV when she was raped.'

'I don't understand,' said Ina.

'No, I don't think you will. It's about – what's the right word, I wonder? – it's about intervention. It's about standing up to what I call the wheels of God.'

'Now I understand even less.'

'Is it necessary that you understand, Ina? Surely what matters is that it was Glenda's decision. It was what she wanted. And unless I'm reading the situation wrongly, it seems to me that you're trying to make your peace with Glenda and with her decisions. Isn't that why you invited me here? And isn't that why you are trying to do something for Sello?'

Ina nodded.

'Well then, don't balk now,' said Sue. 'Don't put the brakes on now.'

Ina made no reply.

A quiet afternoon followed. Sue read to Sello and then they both lay down and dozed off. When Sue woke up, she could hear that the radio was on in Ina's room. In the distance, there was the sound of children kicking a ball. The bedroom was full of languorous shadows. In her fuzzy state, it seemed to Sue that the tenor of the world was sloth, sloth and more sloth; that it was quite obviously so; that the shongololo had read the mood correctly all along. How had the tone ever come to be mistaken for frenzy? Who had announced a juggernaut when there was none? Sello lay curled up next to her; his innocence looked invincible. Sue had never imagined that there could be such serenity in this house of old pain, or in this town, stuck so hastily and with such gross expedience into the ground.

Ina appeared at the door of the bedroom. She spoke softly, so as not to wake Sello. 'Do you want something to eat?'

'I'm still full from that enormous lunch,' said Sue. 'It put me to sleep. I almost never sleep in the afternoons.'

'What about something small? Toasted sandwiches? Does Sello like that?'

'Yes. He does. Thank you.'

Ina walked to the kitchen and Sue could hear her switching on the light and opening the door of the fridge. She should get up, she thought; she should go and help her make the toasted sandwiches. But the effort was too great. Instead, she remained there, listening to Sello's even breathing, lying quite motionless in the room that had now grown dark.

Toothless Tiger

The first animal they saw was a warthog. It snuffled in the sand, right next to the road. They had been anticipating lions and elephants, buffalo and giraffe; they had spoken eagerly of the great creatures they might see, but they found nothing bathetic in the warthog. It was all that they wished for at that moment. They drew up beside it and gazed with wonderment. 'Only his mother could love him,' Paula said. They laughed. They ate dried fruit while they studied the curious animal. Tony had been sleeping in the car and his hair, unruly at the best of times, sprang up unevenly from his pale, rumpled face. But in his eyes – those eyes which Paula found disconcerting, for a boy of fourteen should not have such elderly eyes – there was excitement. She felt refreshed by his delight, by the uncharacteristic display of boyishness.

Something startled the warthog and it ran off into the bush, its tail stiff and erect behind it like a car aerial. This made them laugh again. Even Marcus laughed. Paula was pleased to see that he did not scorn their silly jokes. The holiday mood had taken hold of him too. Was it too much to hope that her father should put aside his habitual sternness for these few days and that her withdrawn son should come out of himself a little? After all, the warthog had charmed them within fifteen minutes of their arrival in the Kruger Park. Marcus, who had seen so many warthogs, and Tony, who had never seen one before – not a real, live one, anyway – were both enchanted by its ugliness. The warthog was a good start.

They arrived at the rest camp just before noon. It was already very hot and, after they checked in, they stumbled with relief into the darkness of their bungalows. Marcus and Tony would share a bungalow, it was decided; Paula would have one to herself. The bungalow had a thatched roof and curtains with an animal pattern in which kudu, wildebeest and impala followed each other with monotonous, hypnotic regularity, like the green-amber-red sequence of a traffic light: each kudu became the promise of a wildebeest, and so on. 'Kitsch,' thought Paula, 'bushveld kitsch'; but she smiled and didn't really mind.

The bungalow was spotlessly clean, there were fresh towels and rectangular little cakes of soap and, best of all, it was cool. Paula always found that heat affected her badly. This was even more so after the years in England. The hot sun took from her; it never seemed to give anything. It was acquisitive, demanding, pushy; she had missed its light when she first went to England, but never its heat. Her mother had been the same: the sun gave her headaches. Paula could remember her lying on her bed on hot summer days with a wet cloth on her forehead, groaning faintly. The only sun-lover in their family was Marcus. His fair skin had made the sun, of necessity, a combatant, but he had never shrunk from the duel. Whenever he could, on weekends and holidays, he had spent his time outdoors. 'You cannot hide from the sun in Africa,' he used to say; and he considered himself a man of Africa. Now, at seventy-eight, he was marked by the sun: his skin was lined and blotchy and his small, pale blue eyes were all that still showed defiance amidst the general surrender of the face. But he didn't care. He had never shown remorse for anything in his life and he was certainly not going to regret the sun. In the end, the sun had kept the gloves on after all, for Marcus had never had skin cancer, although people had always predicted that he would. It was ironic, thought Paula. He had had nearly eight decades of the midday sun, and he did not develop cancer, nor did he go mad, nor – for all his gin-and-tonic sensibility, his leathery colonial air – did he become an Englishman. He had been heedless and he had remained unscathed. And she, who had tried so hard to be solicitous on her own behalf, she with her sunscreen and her pap smears and her mammograms, look what had happened to her. If it were not so tragic, it would be galling.

She could not get away from it: there was no thought of hers that did not lead her back each time to this. It was the snake in the snakes-and-ladders game of her life, the snake that dragged her down again and smirked at the loss of all her ostensible progress. Five years, they told her: five years and she could believe herself to be clear, no more likely to develop it again than someone who has never had it at all. Five years was the target: it would take her out of the terrible game. But she got only as far as three-and-a-half years. This thing which had lain dormant, so quiet that one could begin to believe it was dead; this thing which had had its teeth drawn, or so it seemed; this slumbering thing had woken and it had bitten her again.

She had not told Tony and Marcus yet. She kept waiting for the right time, while the message undelivered weighed heavier and heavier upon her. She had decided she would tell them when they were in the Kruger Park, when they were away from Marcus's big, silent house in Johannesburg – the house she had never felt at home in, the house her mother had never managed to mark with her diffident personality and in which she had died, the house in which Tony lurked and slunk about like an interloper. She had planned to tell them when they were away from that house with its big rooms and slastoed verandahs, its heavy, dark furniture and all its stolid, uncomfortable practicality.

But now she was reluctant to spoil the holiday mood which seemed even to have drawn in Marcus. He had not wanted to leave his home at all: they had great difficulty in persuading him to accompany them, and even greater difficulty persuading themselves that they wanted him to come along, for Paula had never been able to relax in his company and she knew that he made Tony feel tense too. Having got him there, it seemed unfair to strike him with the news of her relapse. Yet she had to tell him before she left for England, for he had the right to hear it in that way, not in a letter or a phone call; and Tony needed to know before then too – in fact, he should have been told already – for the chemotherapy would begin as soon as they got back to London, and he should have time to prepare himself.

She lay on the bed, trying to clear her mind of the stain of thought. Eventually she fell asleep and, when she woke up, the heat had abated. Marcus and Tony were sitting on the verandah of their bungalow, eating naartjies and watching the starlings that flitted about them. 'We were about to come and call you,' said Tony. 'Grandpa says we should go for a drive now that it's getting cooler.'

'Yes,' said Marcus. 'I've been explaining to Tony that in the heat the animals also take a siesta. But now they'll be starting to move around and we'll have a good chance of spotting them, especially around the water-holes.'

They looked at the map of the reserve and chose a looping road that gave them an intermittent view of the river. As she drove, Paula watched Tony in the rear-view mirror, fascinated by his eagerness, yet amused also by the way in which, for all his avid staring out of the window, he spotted almost nothing and had to have the animals pointed out to him by herself or Marcus: a herd of buffalo on the further bank of the river, a great kudu bull with sweeping horns, and even a giraffe that stood right next to the road. 'Look how near he is and I didn't even see him,' said Tony. 'I must have been looking through his legs. Why is it that you and Grandpa always see them and I never do?'

'It's practice,' said Paula. 'You have to get your eye in. You don't really know what you're looking for, that's why you don't see it when it's in front of you. Your eye has to use its prior knowledge to get past the camouflage that the animals use. Grandpa and I have had lots of practice. By the time this holiday is over, you'll be as good as we are – you'll see.'

He tried very hard and he did begin to improve towards the end of the afternoon. They turned around and headed for the camp when the shadows grew long and a cool breeze started up and dispersed some of the thick, warm dusk air. Tony spotted a waterbuck and Paula obligingly stopped the car and reversed so that they could look at it. 'We've seen waterbuck before,' said Marcus. 'We don't have to stop.'

'But Tony spotted this one,' she said. 'He's getting his eye in.'

'We're going to be late,' said Marcus. 'If we get to the camp when the gates are already closed, we'll get a fine.'

'We've got plenty of time, Dad,' she said, starting up the engine nevertheless.

'Step on it!' he said.

She said nothing, but indignation rose up within her, the same old resentment of her childhood and adolescence. His dismissal of Tony's pride in having seen the waterbuck before anyone else did, his assumption that he had the right to give orders, the thin monosyllables that stung her like three little whips – 'Step on it!' – these things woke all the old curdled feelings within her. The monosyllables showed how niggardly and grudging was his authority, as if it could not tolerate even the generosity of a long, full word. Her polysyllabic mind called it antiquated patriarchy; but her sullen heart called it tyranny and she felt it as if she, not Tony, were the smarting child. A few minutes later, when Tony called out again, she stopped the car, even though she heard Marcus sigh with irritation in the seat next to her.

'Go back – quickly!' said Tony.

'What is it?' she asked.

'It's an elephant!' There was great excitement in his voice. They had not yet seen an elephant and, although the big cats were Tony's passion, he was longing to see an elephant too. This elephant, however, was a big grey rock.

'It's a rock!' Marcus said scornfully.

'All right,' Paula said. 'It's easy to make a mistake. That's why camouflage works so well.'

'Now we're definitely going to be late,' he said. 'We'll get a fine because we stopped to look at rocks.'

She drove on angrily while Tony sat silently in the back seat. 'There's a speed limit here,' said Marcus. 'Driving so fast will also get you a fine. Just because your pounds buy you a lot of rands doesn't mean you have to waste them.'

Paula ignored him and drove on as before. They got to the camp with ample time remaining before the gates closed – at least twenty minutes. 'You see,' she said, 'there's plenty of time left.'

'Well, only because you drove as if you were at Kyalami.'

Tony went to look at the curio shop. Paula watched his thin, reedy shape and his sloping gait. A surge of protectiveness passed through her and she cursed herself for having said so little, for having remonstrated so feebly with her father. Why, after all these years, did he still have the power to make her become a child again? He was dried up within himself, but the carapace of him remained, the obdurate shape of his maleness. The substance of his power was gone: in this case the clothes were there but there was no emperor. He was no longer the bank manager, the husband; he was scarcely even the father any more, considering how far away he was and how little he had to do with her life. Yet he still took for granted the entitlement of a brisk instruction or a sharp retort. It never occurred to him that his authority came from somewhere. He simply had it, that was all; and, having had it for most of his life, it never occurred to him that he could ever lose it.

She had never fought against it effectively: at best, her resistance had been sporadic and poorly executed. It was one of the great regrets of her life. But she would not allow him to treat her son in that way. She went to look for her father in his bungalow. He was taking something out of the refrigerator. 'I'm having a beer,' he said. 'Will you join me?'

'I'd love one.' He passed her the beer. After a few moments she said, 'Dad, may I speak to you about something? I would like you to take great care in the way you speak to Tony. He's a sensitive child, you know.' She heard Marcus grunt. 'It hasn't been easy for him since the divorce – I don't have to tell you that. He took it very badly. This holiday is important to him, to both of us. I don't want him to be upset.'

'Let me tell you something,' said Marcus. 'That child, as you call him, is a boy, he is not a child. In fact, he's almost a young man. And the last thing that he needs is to be cossetted. You're doing him harm in treating him as you do. He has an over-protective mother and a father who takes too little interest in him. That, Paula, is a very unhealthy mixture. Very unhealthy.'

'I cannot do anything about his father,' said Paula. 'I can't make him into a different kind of father. But I can make sure that the other people in his life accept that I am the best judge of what is good for him. I must ask you to respect my wishes as a parent.'

'He needs a man. His father is no good and he has no other man in his life.' Paula began to respond to this, but Marcus interrupted her and went on. 'He needs a man to teach him manliness. I'm sorry to tell you this, Paula, but that boy is very girlish.'

'Lower your voice,' she said. 'I can hear footsteps. He might be coming back from the shop.' The footsteps passed by the bungalow and the person walked on. 'I have a different sense of what he needs and what he doesn't,' she began to say; and then Tony appeared after all – his footsteps were so soft that they hadn't even heard him approaching. Paula went to see to their supper. 'Girlish' – what kind of a word was 'girlish'? From what sort of judgement did it proceed? Why should they both – she and Tony – be accused of it in him? She knew that there was what she preferred to call androgyny in the boy, she had seen it at a very early age; and she had ordered herself to welcome it, she had told herself that it was her task to help him to welcome it too, to celebrate it as an unusual configuration within himself. Left to themselves, they could have pulled it off. But they never would be left to themselves to shore up their own definitions, as her father's words reminded her once more. What she wanted Tony to accept in himself became, when her father pronounced upon it, an embarrassing and gaudy thing, interesting only for its exotic appeal, like the skin of a tiger laid out before a hearth, its eyes glassy and its fangs frozen.

They ate quickly and went to bed. They wanted to make an early start: Marcus had told Tony that the morning, before it gets too hot, is good for game-spotting, just as the late afternoon is. The night was crowded with sounds. Something cackled near the camp – a hyena? A jackal? An owl hooted. Moths fluttered against the lights. The air itself seemed to be thick with vigilance. Paula marvelled to think that all this energy renewed itself every night. There was no subsiding; no falling-off; no anti-climax. Against it she set the three of them: a lonely and inflexible old man, a withdrawn and enervated teenager, and a middle-aged woman, threatened by cynicism and cancer, terrified that she would not find the strength to fight the cynicism that she had always held at bay, and that strength would not be enough in the case of the cancer.

The next morning they filled flasks with hot coffee and made sandwiches. They would stop and eat breakfast later: they didn't want to waste precious time now. As soon as the gate of the camp opened, they drove off, turning their heads from left to right, straining still-sleepy eyes to make sure that they missed nothing. They had a good morning. By the time they stopped to eat lunch at a tea room in which a tree grew through the roof, they had seen elephant twice, a large herd of buffalo and many of the more common species, including scores of giraffe and a troop of baboons. Yet Tony was disappointed. He was playing lackadaisically with his food. Paula saw that he was getting more pimples. His body, in which he lived ever more awkwardly as he grew older, was turning on him and nipping at him, leaving red marks. He seemed to need to be protected even from the malice of his own body. Paula knew the reason for his disappointment. 'Don't worry,' she said. 'We have two more days in the park. We may still see some of the big cats.'

'I hope so,' Tony said. 'I would love to see a lion. Or a tiger. Or a leopard. Or a cheetah.'

Paula hoped that Marcus hadn't heard. She would correct the mistake gently. But he did hear and he was too quick for her. 'For heaven's sake,' he said. 'Where do you think we are? In India? There are no tigers in Africa. Don't you know that?'

'That will do, Dad,' said Paula. 'Don't make a big deal out of it.'

'But tigers,' he said. 'Tigers, of all things!'

Paula prepared wearily to do battle. She had to force herself to do so. Her quarrels with her father had a mechanistic quality about them now; they fought as if by rote. She was tired of old fights, of going over the same old territory. Regression seemed to have become her fate, push forward as she might: was it any wonder that it was becoming easier to be cynical?

Then, before she could speak, she heard Tony's voice. 'I'm sorry, Grandpa,' he said. 'But I don't live in Africa, like you. I don't know these things. I'm trying to learn. I think you should help me to learn, instead of snapping at me when I get things wrong.'

Paula was astonished. She could see that Marcus was too. He made no reply, which meant that Tony had won. Marcus never apologised: it was something that he simply didn't do, and expecting him to apologise was like expecting him to do embroidery – it would never happen. But his silence meant that he had no way of countering the remark. Tony's voice had wavered a little as he spoke, but he had prepared his response and seen it through to its conclusion. Paula was proud of him. He had stood up to her father. He had done it. He had acted like a man – no, it was better than that: he had acted like the man she wanted him to become.

They returned to the camp. The midday heat meant that they saw almost nothing. When they got back, they made for the coolness of the bungalows. They would have a siesta, as they did the day before – it was the best way to deal with the worst hours of the heat. As Paula lay down on the bed, a loud noise startled her. Someone had turned a radio on and was playing it loudly. The noise came from the bungalow behind theirs. She lay there, filled with resentment. Then she heard a voice raised in anger. It was Marcus's. She got up and went outside. Marcus had set off in pursuit of the offending noise and was now yelling at two barefoot and shirtless young men. 'Turn the damn thing off!' he was saying. 'Where do you think you are – on the beach?'

'Don't you like it?' said one of the young men. 'Not your kind of music?' He leaned against the door of their bungalow, smiling archly, winking at his friend, languorous as a well-fed cat. He held the radio – an enormous ghetto-blaster – in his hand.

'No, I don't like it!' said Marcus. His anger made the red and white blotches on his face stand out more starkly. 'It's disturbing everyone. Turn it off now or I'll call the authorities.'

'Oh, please Sir, don't do that,' said the young man. 'I'm so frightened of that.' He played with his chin and winked again at his friend, who said, 'Keep your hair on – the bit that you've got left.' Then they both laughed. Marcus moved closer towards them. The first young man, without changing his position, leaned forward and turned the radio down slightly. 'Is that better?' he asked, running his tongue along his top lip, lowering his voice so that they could hardly hear it. It was not much better. Paula saw Marcus hesitate, then he said, 'Yes. Now just keep it down. I don't want to have to come and speak to you again.' Paula saw the young man push his hand down the front of his shorts. He left it there and stared boldly at them. She turned away.

She regretted bitterly that she had witnessed the confrontation. Marcus had met them with his customary assurance, a man going out to scold the boys, and they had made an old codger out of him. He had used what he had always relied upon before, but now it was not enough. The snapping young males had challenged the aged leader of the pack and forced him to face his own toothlessness. To see his pride so lacerated was painful. It was impossible not be moved, for Marcus knew no other way; therefore he had nothing else.

'I gave them a piece of my mind,' he said.

'Did you, Dad? Good for you,' said Paula. The music had been turned up again and was as loud as before, if not worse. But they ignored it and behaved as if Marcus had accomplished something. To get away from it, they set off on their afternoon drive earlier than they intended, even though it was still hot. Only Tony had been able to sleep through the noise. In the car Tony and Marcus were both very quiet and, after they had driven for half an hour and seen nothing, Paula glanced to the side and saw that Marcus's eyes were closed. She looked in the rear-view mirror and saw that Tony was also asleep. She stopped the car rather suddenly, so that they both woke up. 'Excuse me,' she said. 'Do I have to drive and look for the animals? There could be a big cat right next to the road and you two wouldn't even see it.'

'To see as much as we have and still to be dissatisfied is ridiculous,' said Marcus. 'The big cats are not everything. You should not tolerate these whims and this sort of precious behaviour.'

Paula didn't respond. Tony sighed and stared glassily out of the window. She could see that all the excitement he had felt at the beginning of this holiday was gone. He was again what he was at home: too desultory even to be moody, so undemanding that she sometimes wanted to take him by his thin shoulders and push him towards a desire, a resolution, even an act of hostility – anything. The holiday, having roused him at first, was now casting him down and there was more to it than simply not having been lucky enough to see lions or leopards or cheetahs. On top of this, she would have to tell him the news of the relapse. What all this made clear to her was that there was no way of protecting him: to believe that one could shield him from anything at all was absurd – it was the worst kind of delusion.

Eventually it grew slightly cooler. 'We'd better start making our way back,' said Marcus. 'We're far from the camp.' Paula consulted the map and chose a road that would return them to the camp and take in several water-holes on the way. After forty minutes, they suddenly came upon about a dozen cars parked at all angles in the road. People had stuck their heads out of the car windows and were passing binoculars to one another. Paula drew up alongside them.

'What is it?' called Tony from the back seat.

'I can't see anything,' said Paula. 'But it must be the big cats. Nothing else would draw so many cars.'

'What have you got?' Marcus asked the man in the car next to them.

'Lions!' said the man. 'A male and two females and some cubs.

They crossed the road a few hours ago and they've been lying under those trees since then. Everyone is waiting for them to get up again.'

Tony begged her to drive closer to the side of the road. It was difficult to do so, but eventually one of the other cars pulled out and they had an opportunity to move forward. Tony peered through the binoculars and, with a whoop of excitement, declared that he could see the lions. Paula looked through the binoculars too. Yes, there they were: she could see little more than a flicking ear and, for a few seconds, the outline of a head through the shrub; but they were certainly there. More cars began to leave. 'We have to go,' said Marcus. 'We've got a long way to go and it's getting late.'

'Please, Mum,' said Tony. 'Just a bit longer. They might stand up.' He so seldom called her 'Mum' these days.

'Step on it!' said Marcus. More cars pulled away: there were only four left now. Marcus peered at his watch and glared at them both. Paula ignored him and looked at Tony through the rear-view mirror. He had his head out of the window but drew it in to look at her with tacit gratitude when he saw that she was not obeying. She felt exultant, for she and Tony were together in this, they were sharing the defiance, her father could grumble and threaten all he liked, but they were not going to budge. There was now only one other car. The late afternoon grew cool and shadowy as the stultifying heat abandoned its grip. Suddenly Paula drew her breath in with a gasp. By the side of the road, materialising as if from nowhere, stood one of the lionesses. Paula leaned back and shook Tony. Then she pointed at the lioness and gestured that he should be quiet. She studied the rapt expression on his face with joy.

The other car drew away. Shortly afterwards the second lioness and two cubs appeared at the side of the road. Marcus, looking at his watch again, said to Paula, 'You're too old to be so stupid. Do you think it's clever to teach your son to break rules?'

'Perhaps there's a place for it sometimes,' murmured Paula. He made no reply. The pride of lions crossed the road in front of them: first the lionesses and the cubs, then the great black-maned male. It was too dark to take photographs, so they simply watched the unhurried progress of the animals. The lions moved slowly towards the river and then vanished from sight. Paula started the car, switched on the lights and drove off. She put her foot on the accelerator. They were still on the sand road and clouds of dust rose up beside and behind them. They drove in silence, but occasionally she had glimpses of the faces of the others. It was almost amusing to see the contrast. Tony was in a state of bliss – there was no other way to describe his silly grin. Marcus's face was wooden with impotent anger. 'Never mind,' she thought. 'You will learn nothing from this, of course; you will merely be confirmed in the staleness of being right, always right. But I don't care.'

There was a great thud and the steering-wheel shuddered in her hand. They had collided with something. Paula slammed on the brakes as the car began to veer to the side. They stopped and she opened her door, afraid to get out. Something was lying on the road, something that twitched and jerked and kicked its legs. She walked slowly towards it. Marcus and Tony stayed in the car, but Tony called out, 'Be careful, Mum! It's dangerous. Be careful!'

When she drew nearer, she saw that it was an impala. Its neck was twisted under its body and the spasmodic movements were already becoming more irregular. It was dying, if not dead already. She walked back to the car and inspected the damage. The front was badly dented in and one of the head-lights was broken. She got behind the wheel again and slammed the door shut. 'There's no use staying here,' she said to Tony. 'It's dead.'

'It looks injured,' he whispered.

'No. It's dead. That's just the rigor mortis.'

They drove away. She prepared herself for an onslaught from Marcus, but he said nothing. She thought grimly of the impala. It would be eaten tonight by predators. That would have been its fate sooner or later anyway. She was prepared to deal ruthlessly with it, even in her thoughts, where under different circumstances there might have been contrition. For all its bushveld kitsch, the curio shops, the cameras and binoculars, the safety of being in cars and within the rest camps, this was still a place of tooth and claw. She, in her benevolent curiosity and her rented car, she too had killed. She had killed, harmless as she was. In a curious way, she did not regret it. She had her young to protect.

They got to the camp as the gates were being closed. The guard smiled at them and opened the gates again to let them through. Paula gave him a thumbs-up sign and called out, 'Thank you!' He did not seem to notice the damage to the car, or else he thought nothing of it.

She parked the car and they got out. Marcus and Tony began to walk to their bungalow, but she called them back. A strange calm passed over her. She felt powerful, in charge; her eye was in. 'Please come into my bungalow for a minute,' she said. 'I have something to tell you both.'

The Tracks of Hidden Things

Everyone told Gary the same thing: you'll get nowhere with the husband. He's a cul-de-sac. Marshall? Forget it. Others have tried and failed. He won't budge. He's the archetypal control freak. Talk about anal-retentive! Speak to him by all means – just don't get your hopes up. Marshall is the widower from Hell.

Consequently, when Gary went to see Professor Edgar Marshall in Oxford, he did not dare to hope for more than a creditable defeat. He needed to know that he had tried, but, on the strength of their correspondence regarding the disputed manuscripts as well as the experiences of other researchers, he expected the appeal to fail. Nonetheless, he felt a grudging curiosity. He wanted to meet the man whom all the literary world loathed. Every day biographers, editors, critics and publishers prayed earnestly and in touching sincerity for Marshall's death. An obliging God, one who was open to supplication and who felt even a jot of compassion for these frustrated people, would have been pleased to terminate at once the obstructionist life of Professor

Marshall. But there was either too little compassion or too much perversity: Professor Marshall remained alive, vigorous and litigious. He watched over his wife's estate with an implacable vigilance.

The worst part of it, as people kept saying, was that Marshall had such archaic ideas about literature. He lumbered about like a brontosaurus in a shopping mall. He knew so little that he had no sense of how little he knew. There could not have been a more inappropriate custodian. In becoming the executor of his late wife's estate, he appointed himself also the Keeper of her Reputation. He permitted only what he deemed worthy to be published: the rest of the material – and there was a great deal that Etta Cook had left unpublished at her death – he suppressed. He put out an edition of her *Selected Letters*, but made it clear that the *Collected Letters* would not be contemplated, nor would the *Collected Works*. Nothing that he considered inferior would be allowed to detract from the acknowledged masterpieces. He would keep the Cook canon pure.

In numerous discussions, some of them taking place in university common rooms, others in private homes over a glass of wine, people returned again and again to the subject of Marshall and the Cook estate. What, they asked each other despairingly, did Marshall think a canon was? What principle of selection was he applying? What crude and antiquated notion, what misguided passion drove him to suppress so much material that ought to be made available? What gave him the right to convert the smorgasbord of Etta Cook's life and work into a set menu with very small portions? And there was another grievance, equally substantial: it was grossly unjust that an elderly British man with no connection to South Africa other than the fact that he had been married to Etta Cook for the last years of her life should be in a position to control the estate of someone whose early work, at least, marked her as an important South African writer.

Gary had never been in England in the winter before: the jittery sun slipped away after a few pallid hours and, although it was only three o'clock in the afternoon, he was dismayed to find that it was already dark. Professor Marshall lived in North Oxford, close to Port Meadow. His house was long and narrow: five storeys high, with only one or two rooms on each floor. Gary was ushered into the sitting-room, where cats blinked at them from every corner. Marshall did not at all resemble the man Gary had prepared himself for: the failure of the mental picture he had drawn, based in particular on the curt and dismissive letters he had received, was disconcerting. He had been expecting a tall, thin man, suspicious and uncommunicative, the pale, dry exterior barely concealing the fanaticism with which he exercised his custodianship. Instead Gary found a short, florid man with a paunch and a bald head, who welcomed him in an effusive manner, gave him little or no opportunity to speak and seemed like a cross between Mr Micawber and Dr Doolittle.

'Another young man from South Africa!' Marshall called out. 'There's no shortage of them. I must tell you I have a soft spot for these young South Africans. I always did, even when we were supposed to avoid them like the plague. They seemed such fine fellows. I felt sorry for them. After Etta and I were married, we often invited them to dinner. After all, they weren't to blame for what the government was doing. But now we're allowed to welcome you with open arms! And we can buy your fruit and wine without getting dirty looks from people. I shall expect you to tell me all the latest news. I wish Etta had lived to see the transformation! Do you know that, during the years of our marriage, we used to spend several months every year in South Africa?'

'Where?' asked Gary, feeling that it was wise, where possible, to restrict his interjections to single words.

'We had a holiday home at Hermanus. I suppose you know it? Lovely part of the world. Quite spectacular. Nothing like where Etta grew up: it's all sea and mountains, much more European than the Transvaal. I think that's why she liked it. Sherry?'

Gary didn't realise at first that the last word meant he was being offered something, but then he saw that Professor Marshall was inclining a decanter in the direction of two small glasses. He accepted the sherry and sank into a bumpy chair that needed new upholstering. Marshall drew a cat onto his lap and looked at Gary through thick-lensed glasses. 'We used to go to Namaqualand for the wild flowers,' he said. 'Etta was passionate about them. You've been there, I presume?'

'Professor Marshall,' said Gary, 'may I ask you about the material that has recently come to light as a result of the Brink bequest? You will recall our correspondence.'

'Ah, yes,' said Marshall. 'Business first, of course. You brisk young people haven't got time to sit around and natter. Now let me remind myself: you're referring to some papers that have been left to the university library. Cape Town, wasn't it?'

'Wits,' said Gary.

'I've had many requests in the past regarding the material that is housed in that library,' said Marshall. 'I've indicated that, unfortunately, I cannot sanction its publication. It's not up to scratch. Very disappointing to everyone, I'm sure. I'm afraid there are a lot of people who are not pleased with me. Not pleased at all.' He smiled coyly and for a second an impish boy peeped out from behind the fleshy face.

Gary said, 'You may remember from our correspondence that I

am not referring to the papers that have been housed in the library for many years. I have in mind the new material that has come to us from the estate of Louise Brink, who was a friend of Miss Cook – of Mrs Marshall – during her years in Johannesburg, before she left for the UK. The papers were left in a box in Mrs Brink's care and they were never reclaimed.'

'Louise Brink,' said Marshall. 'Yes, I met her once or twice. So she's died, eh? She lived near the zoo – what's that suburb called? Westcliff? Johannesburg has beautiful suburbs. Not such an ugly city after all, if you know where to go. Very good climate, too. Is it as dangerous now as people say? We hear dreadful stories.'

Gary drew in his breath and went on. 'What we have found is extremely exciting,' he said. 'You may recall that I sent you a copy of some of this new material. As I have indicated, there are eight chapters of an incomplete novel, what seems to be part of another novel, as well as several shorter pieces.'

'I've got bad news for you,' said Marshall. 'It's not genuine. Undoubtedly not authentic. I would have known about it. Etta would have mentioned it. She never once indicated that Louise Brink had anything in her possession. I'm afraid you're wasting your time. In any case, I could see from what you were kind enough to photocopy for me that it is not her handwriting.'

'On the contrary,' said Gary. 'We have consulted several handwriting experts. Although the handwriting is a little different from the mature script you are familiar with, they have all assured us that it is the same hand.' Marshall smiled and sipped his sherry. Gary went on: 'Although these are early works – juvenilia, in some cases – I believe that they are extremely important, Professor Marshall. The incomplete novel, for a start, takes on the question of race relations in an uncannily prophetic way. It would be of great interest to people for historical as well as literary reasons. This new material would add substantially to the existing body of work and, in particular, to that part of it which is South African in content or orientation. It would make Etta Cook an even more important South African writer than she already is. It would enhance her reputation.'

'More sherry?' Marshall reached for the decanter again.

'Thank you, I haven't quite finished the first glass,' said Gary.

'This cat is called Gibbon,' said Marshall, indicating the one on his lap, although Gary hadn't said anything about cats. 'Then we've got Macaulay, Arnold, Newman, Ruskin and Browning. Carlyle died last month. Some of them are girls, but they all have boys' names.' He chuckled and tilted his head. Then he said, 'With due respect, you must remember that whereas ambitious young scholars like yourself are out to make a great literary find and advance your careers – and I don't blame you for it, why shouldn't you? – my job is to protect Etta and her reputation. That is my only concern and even when people get cross with me, ever so cross, I never lose sight of that. That is why I cannot allow anything of dubious quality or questionable authenticity to appear under her name.' He stroked the cat called Gibbon, his plump white hand moving all the way from its head to its tail.

Gary could see that his defeat was going to be complete, not creditable, probably ignominious. 'Literary reputations are not fixed,' he said. 'They change all the time.'

'That may be,' said Marshall. 'However, I cannot allow such considerations to affect me in any way. I have to carry out my responsibilities and look after what has been entrusted to me. Who else has Etta got to look after her interests?'

After that, there seemed to be nothing to say. Gary put on his coat and began to move towards the door. Suddenly he remembered that there was one thing more that he wanted to ask. 'By the way, there's a loose page amongst the manuscripts that came to us from the Brink estate that I can't fathom at all,' he said. 'I didn't send it to you with the rest of the photocopies, but perhaps you wouldn't mind looking at it now? It intrigues me. The handwriting is the same, but it doesn't seem to belong with the rest of the material.'

'Let's have a look,' said Professor Marshall, smiling broadly. He studied the sheet of paper while Gary, who knew it by heart, looked at it again over his shoulder. There were a number of words and phrases, scattered irregularly over the page. At the top and the bottom the phrase *the tracks of hidden things* appeared. There were also the words *white films*, *evil demon*, *seven husbands* and *gall*.

'Might be some sort of code,' said Prof Marshall. 'Very peculiar. Certainly not the kind of thing Etta would go in for.'

'You don't know what it means?'

'Beats me.' He returned the sheet of paper. At the door, Gary thanked him for his time. 'Don't mention it,' said Marshall. 'I'll be pleased to see you if you're in this part of the world again.' He twinkled and grew conspiratorial. 'And I'll be even more pleased if you bring me some of your wonderful dried fruit – especially peaches and mangoes and guavas!'

The air was chilly and damp as Gary walked back through Jericho to the centre of town. Little clouds of dandelion mist clustered around the street lamps. He looked at the colleges as he passed them and wished he knew which was which, but they seldom displayed the names outside the college buildings. The implication was plain: you ought to know already which college it was; if you didn't then your ignorance disqualified you from knowledge. The sense of tradition and entrenchment which people always spoke of was undoubtedly present, but its effect on him was alienating. He felt that there was no word that he could utter in this place, no dialogue in which he could seek a lodging. That was what the old buildings seemed to be saying; it was certainly the message that he had received from Professor Marshall.

Yet this was where Etta Cook had spent her last years. He had hoped that being here and meeting her husband would have helped him to understand better the curious, looping trajectory of her life. Instead, it receded even further from his grasp. He could not get his mind around it: the incongruities drifted like a miasma over his attempts to frame her life and represent it to himself. He could not make her compatible with herself.

For a start, there were so many lacunae. Evidently, her journey took in what he thought of as three discrete lives and three names. The first life consisted of pig-tails and bare feet, dusty veld, mealies (usually withering), church pews and long sermons. It also included hours at the barre under the tutelage of Miss Oldman, who taught the Royal Academy of Dancing syllabus. Gary felt he knew what Miss Oldman must have looked and sounded like: pinched and shrill, a pickled cucumber of a woman, an English spinster living in an Afrikaans town, dreaming, no doubt, of Kew Gardens and mistletoe and Queen Anne's Lace. This first life of Etta's was called Henrietta Koekemoer and it ended when she defied her father and left for Johannesburg.

The second life seemed to have only the ballet in common with the first. Etta was a gifted dancer and Miss Oldman had given her a good training. From Johannesburg she went to London. Injury ended the ballet career after eighteen months. In the years that followed, there were two husbands (the first of whom lasted a fortnight) and a child, possibly fathered by someone else, who was born with spina bifida and lived for only a short time. There were rumours of lovers and scandalous affairs, but Marshall's edition of the *Selected Letters* revealed nothing. There were well-documented trips to India, China and Mexico; there was a villa in Tuscany in which she lived with the second husband, who was wealthy. Few photographs survived, although it was thought that Marshall had others in his possession. Etta left the second husband and returned to London. There were periods in which she wrote and published, others – some of them lasting for years – in which she seemed not to write at all. This second life was called Etta Cook and it ended in the marriage to Professor Edgar Marshall.

The third life began with the astonishment of everyone who had ever known Etta Cook. The marriage was the least predictable act of an unpredictable life. To one as restless and iconoclastic as Etta, marriage to Marshall, they argued, would be stifling. They waited for her to suffer the inevitable claustrophobia, to chafe against it and then to claim her freedom. But she did not do so. She gave no indication of being unhappy. Her views seemed to become more conservative, which disappointed many of her admirers. She wrote very little and lived quietly in Oxford, spending part of the English winter in South Africa. This life was called Mrs Edgar Marshall and it ended with her sudden death at the age of sixty-four.

That was what was known or surmised. But Gary could not ascertain what lay within the thin outer casing of facts and rumours. Back in Johannesburg, he found that his preoccupation with Etta Cook deepened. What he couldn't understand had begun by challenging him, but now it rebuked him. He felt, irrationally, that the cryptic words and phrases on the loose sheet of paper would yield the answer to the mysteries, but he came no closer to understanding what they meant. Was it the core of a novel which was never written? Was it indeed a sort of code, as Marshall had suggested? Who or what was the evil demon? What were white films? What did gall signify? Who, except for Elizabeth Taylor, had ever had seven husbands? To what did the hidden tracks of things lead?

He wrote again to Professor Marshall about the Brink bequest, hoping that their meeting in Oxford would count for something. He asked Marshall whether he would be prepared to appoint scholars and handwriting experts of his own to assess the manuscripts. He stressed that he had no doubt in his mind that the material was genuine and offered further evidence in support of this, such as the fact that characters from the abandoned novel re-appeared in works published some years later. All he received in reply was a letter from Marshall's solicitors, stressing that no questionable, unpublished or archival material could be made available to the public at large without the written permission of Professor Edgar Marshall, sole heir and executor of the estate of Etta Cook. In this instance, Professor Marshall had decided to exercise his legal prerogative: researchers could consult the papers in the university archives, but none of the material could be considered for publication.

The less success Gary had, the more determined he became not to give up. He saw his obsession for what it was and did nothing to stop it. In moments of unsparing honesty, he asked himself what the difference was between himself and Marshall: after all, they both wished to exercise control over the Cook estate; they both had an idea of Etta Cook, a version of her, as it were, that they considered superior to others' and that they wished to convey to the world. He liked to believe that his version was more comprehensive and more generous: that, for all his vast ignorance and Etta Cook's elusiveness, it nonetheless came closer to the quirkiness and complexity of her life and work, whereas Marshall was maiming her in the act of protecting her. But he wondered whether the distinction was as profound as he liked to believe. He hated to think that he had anything in common with a man for whom zeal was a straitjacket. But who was to say? The fact that he recognised his less-than-innocent motives, while Marshall did not, could not exonerate him. In the end, what he sought impotently to do was no less morbid than what Marshall had the power to do. They both depended upon the malleability of the dead. But the dead, he reflected, are as recalcitrant as they are malleable: their silence and their words are double-edged.

Whatever the page of cryptic words might mean, Gary believed that he could read in it Etta Cook's defiance – her refusal to submit to Marshall, to himself, to all those who sought to exercise power over her. She had written those words at a time when her posthumous fate would have been the last thing on her mind, yet the enigma they held was now shielding her. Something from her youth had come solicitously to her defence in the end. The inversion was typical: nothing in her life ever seemed to be straightforward; nothing would oblige a pattern that others sought to impose.

That very realisation provided the first clue to the mystery Gary had struggled with for so long. Suddenly he knew that he had been looking in the wrong place: he had doggedly sought a linear path when the track that he was following had an entirely different shape. Preoccupied as he was with the destination, he had not taken cognisance of the route. He had gone to the end of her life, to Marshall, to the house in Oxford in which she had died, in the mistaken belief that it would yield the vantage-point from which he could look back and see her life laid out before him. His thinking was at fault, hopelessly at fault: it should have been as skewed and circuitous as that which he wished to follow. He had tried to read the sibylline words as if they obeyed some kind of sequential order, but that was precisely what they would not do. They were like fallen leaves, full of wind-whimsy, mad with the zigzag of hither and thither.

One morning he filled his car with petrol and set off, heading in an easterly direction. It was a curious journey, for he neither knew precisely what he sought nor where to look for it. All he had was the feather of a wild goose.

The road was crowded with vehicles. Normally a placid driver, he found himself enraged that morning by the fact that he had to keep slowing down. There were trucks crawling along in the fast lane and it seemed to him, in that short-lived paranoia that being behind the wheel of a car sometimes induces, that they were deliberately thwarting his progress. It was hot and he could seldom go fast enough to feel the relief of a breeze. All the frustration that had built up in recent months boiled within him. Some of it had been caused by Marshall, who would not cede control; some of it came from Etta Cook herself, who would not give up her secrets; most of it, however, was the result of his own inability to let go of the tangled business and move on. He found himself swinging recklessly from one lane to another, relishing the indignant hooting that ensued as if it were applause.

The town in which Etta had gone to school and had her ballet lessons was obscure, hot, and dusty. Only the wide main street was tarred and it was interrupted at regular intervals by stop signs, for there was not a single traffic light. Gary found the municipal offices and made enquiries about the Koekemoer family and the farm

Onverwacht. A slow-moving woman did her best to help. There were no more Koekemoers in the area, he was told; there hadn't been for twenty years. The farm had been bought and sold many times since they left.

'Why are you looking for the Koekemoers?' the woman asked. 'Are they relatives of yours?'

'No,' said Gary. 'I'm trying to trace someone's life – find out more about it.'

'Well, good luck,' she said.

He turned to leave and then, on an impulse, he reached in his pocket for the photocopy of the sheet of cryptic words and showed it to her. 'Does this mean anything to you?'

She read the words out loud, slowly and ponderously. 'White fil-lums,' she said. 'Evil de-mon. What does it mean?'

'Never mind,' said Gary. 'It's not important.' He cursed his foolishness. How could this woman possibly know anything? For that matter, what secrets could this town hold, spread open as it was beneath the sun, as exposed as a peeled fruit? The Koekemoers had gone and Etta had taken her secrets with her.

Something else occurred to him. 'I don't suppose anyone in this town will still remember Miss Oldman, the ballet teacher?' he asked. 'She must have died too long ago for even the elderly residents to have known her.'

'Miss Oldman? She's not dead. Why didn't you tell me you wanted to speak to her? I'll give you her address.'

'She's *alive*? But how can it be? She must be well over a hundred years old!'

'Not at all – she's about eighty, although she looks much younger. I'm sure she would love to have someone to talk to about the old days.'

Gary did some calculations as he walked to the car. Another mental picture had failed him: Miss Oldman, when she taught Etta ballet, must have been a young woman in her early thirties.

He realised that he was hungry: he hadn't eaten anything since early that morning and it was now mid-afternoon. In a restaurant where he was the only customer, he ate lamb cutlets and mashed potato mixed with beans while someone swept the floor around his feet. Then he set off in pursuit of Miss Oldman.

She lived in a small house just off the main road. Her garden was colourful, although there was no flower bed: hibiscus, bottle-brush, Pride of India and hydrangea supplied all the colour. Miss Oldman was a tall woman who did indeed seem far younger than she was – the ballet mistress's posture, the straight back and unhesitating steps, contributed to that impression. Her house was cool and very quiet: the loudest sounds were the ticking of a clock and the frustration of a fly against the fly-screen.

'Please forgive the intrusion,' said Gary, noticing immediately that there were several photographs of Etta Cook in the sitting-room and more in the dining-room. In one a young girl in a leotard stood in first position and smiled shyly at the camera. In another, Etta and Miss Oldman were feeding pigeons: the great black rump of a lion behind them signalled that it was Trafalgar Square.

'Nothing to forgive,' said Miss Oldman. 'Anyone who is interested in Etta will always be welcome here.'

She was not, after all, small or shrill. Although English-speaking, there was nothing British about her or her accent.

Some of the photographs were taken recently: there was even one of Etta and Professor Marshall sitting under a beach umbrella. Others, inscribed 'To MGO, with love' by Etta, marked the stages of her lionisation: she posed at award ceremonies in the company of the judges or with other famous writers. Gary had imagined that, in her platteland isolation, Miss Oldman would have been ignorant of the subsequent career of Etta Cook, but he saw now how wrong he was. She had conscientiously followed the course of Etta's fame and they had kept in touch throughout the years: they had even exchanged letters the week before Etta died. He had believed that, in her determination to shake off the Highveld dust forever, Etta would have wanted nothing to do with any part of her first life. Yet she had corresponded with Miss Oldman for over forty years. It made him realise again how every construction he tried to place on her life seemed to be untenable.

Miss Oldman gave him the history of each photograph. Several of them dated from the two trips she had made to Europe to visit her friend: once when Etta was living in a flat in Hampstead and once when she was in the villa in Tuscany.

'I met all sorts of famous people,' she said. 'The person I really wanted to meet was Ninette De Valois, and Henrietta said she would try and arrange it, but she never managed to do so. But I did meet Noel Coward. And Francis Bacon.'

Gary smiled to think of the ballet mistress from the platteland moving in those Bohemian and Continental circles. Miss Oldman had also gone down to the coast one Christmas to visit Etta and Professor Marshall in Hermanus. All of this showed an unexpected willingness on Etta's part to bring together the various parts of her life: perhaps the scheme of the three discrete lives which he had fashioned was more convenient than accurate?

What he learned very quickly about Miss Oldman was that she was extremely religious. There were tracts on the walls and a large gold cross hung about her neck. Ballet and religion had been the two disciplines of her life. Eventually she retired from the former and the young girls of the town no longer passed through her hands. But this gave her more time for the latter: in the course of their conversation, she mentioned church bazaars, fetes and a campaign to raise funds for a new church hall.

'Yet Etta was a complete atheist, was she not?' Gary asked.

Miss Oldman sighed. 'That's because they forced it down her throat as a child,' she said. 'They ruined it for her. That's not the way to bring children to religion.'

'Her atheism was not a source of conflict between you?'

'Oh, no. I can tell you that Henrietta was a very spiritual woman. When she died, I took comfort in the fact that God would not turn His face away from a soul as spiritual and kind as that.'

'You feel you knew her well?'

'Yes, indeed. First as my pupil, then as my friend.'

'Then how do you account for the marriage to Professor Marshall? Most people who knew her found it surprising, to say the least.'

'But that is because they didn't know her father – the late Mr Koekemoer. I did know him. And I could see that the Professor reminded Henrietta of him. After rebelling against her father all her life, it was a relief to her to stop quarrelling, to make peace. Her last years were tranquil years. And the Professor was always very kind to me.'

'Well, he's making a lot of trouble now,' said Gary, resenting the tribute to Marshall. 'People hate him because he controls her estate and won't allow some of the material to be made available.'

'They shouldn't hate him,' said Miss Oldman, shaking her head. 'That's not right. They should be grateful to him for caring about her.'

This was an entirely new approach. Gary didn't know quite how to respond to it. Instead, as it was growing late and he would have to drive home in the dark, he unfolded the copy of the loose page and said, 'Miss Oldman, you have been most helpful. May I ask you one more thing? Would you mind looking at this? It's something that Etta scribbled down many years ago and it's recently come to light. I can't make head or tail of it. Does it mean anything to you?'

Miss Oldman studied the sheet and then made a clicking sound. 'Typical,' she said. 'That naughty girl. So typical.'

'Do you mean you know what it is?'

'Of course.'

'Could you enlighten me? It would put me out of my misery.'

'It's from the book called *Tobit* – at least, most of it seems to be. That's where the evil demon comes from and the white films and the fish's gall.' She smiled benignly.

'Miss Oldman,' said Gary. 'Dear Miss Oldman. Forgive me. I haven't the faintest idea what you're talking about.'

'Oh, I beg your pardon. I always assume that people will be able to follow scriptural references. I shouldn't do that.'

'It's from the Bible? Are you telling me it's from the Bible?' He was amazed: he had considered countless allusive possibilities, but the Bible had never crossed his mind. Why would Etta, whose atheism was part of her early rebellion, turn to the Bible? It didn't make sense.

'No, no,' said Miss Oldman, shaking her head. 'It's not the Bible. That's the whole point. It's an apocryphon. The book called *Tobit* is one of the Old Testament Apocrypha. The Apocrypha are those books that were not accepted into the Bible. That's why I said Henrietta was naughty. She knew that these are the rejected writings. Wait, I'll show you.'

She excused herself and went into the next room. When she returned, she smiled encouragingly. 'I found it,' she said. 'This copy of the Old Testament has the Apocrypha at the end – as an appendix. Here, let's sit at the table and I'll put the lamp on.'

Gary sat next to her and they bent their heads over the book. Together they read the story of Tobit who, in defiance of the Assyrians, insists on burying the dead in secret. On one occasion, he sleeps outside because he has been defiled by contact with a corpse:

> *I slept by the wall of the courtyard, and my face was uncovered. I did not know that there were sparrows on the wall and their fresh droppings fell into my open eyes and white films formed on my eyes. I went to physicians, but they did not help me.*

They read also of Sarah, a young woman living at Ecbatana in Media, who contemplates suicide because she had been given in marriage seven times and, on each occasion, the evil demon Asmodeus slew her husband before the consummation of the marriage. In her anguish she prays to God, saying, 'Already seven husbands of mine are dead. Why should I live?' Tobias, the son of Tobit, is sent to Media to retrieve some money for his father. The angel Raphael is sent to accompany Tobias:

> *And Raphael was sent to heal the two of them: to scale away the white films from Tobit's eyes; to give Sarah the daughter of Raguel in marriage to Tobias the son of Tobit, and to bind Asmodeus the evil demon.*

Tobias catches a fish in the Tigris River and Raphael (whom he doesn't know to be an angel) tells him to 'cut open the fish and take the heart and liver and gall and put them away safely.' By burning the heart and liver in live ashes of incense, Tobias banishes Asmodeus the evil demon and is able to marry Sarah – this time she manages to consummate her marriage. When they return to Assyria, Tobias anoints his father's blind eyes with the gall of the fish: the white films fall away and Tobit's eyesight is restored.

Then Gary flipped through the other books of the Apocrypha and, in the book called *Sirach*, which consists of a long poem, his eye fell on something which made him whoop with delight. Miss Oldman patted his shoulder affectionately. 'Don't get too excited,' she said; but he could see that she was enjoying his enthusiasm. He showed her what he had found:

For the Most High knows all that
may be known,
and he looks into the signs of
the age.
He declares what has been and
what is to be,
and he reveals the tracks of hidden things.

Miss Oldman didn't keep anything strong in the house, but they celebrated with a bottle of apple cider. 'It has very little alcohol in it,' said Miss Oldman, opening it with a wink. She invited Gary to stay for supper, but he said he had to get back: it was already dark and he had a long way to go. 'Let me give you some prickly pears, then,' she said. 'They grow in my back yard.'

'I've never eaten prickly pears,' said Gary.

'Ah, you don't know what you're missing.' She fetched some from the fridge – 'you must chill them first' – and showed him how to peel them without getting thorns in his fingers.

'An unusual taste,' said Gary, chewing one carefully. 'Very delicate.' Miss Oldman persuaded him to eat two more.

Standing at his car, he said, 'I can't thank you enough.'

'Bless you,' she replied. 'Come and visit again.'

'I would like to. I suppose you've kept the letters Etta wrote to you over the years?'

'Every one.'

'Would you consider letting me look at them?'

'Yes. I would.'

He started the car, rolled down the window and shouted, 'Thanks for the prickly pears! I'll be in touch.'

As busy as the road had been that morning, so quiet was it now. There was scarcely another vehicle to be seen as Gary sped along the highway, the tar making gritty, spitting little sounds beneath the wheels of his car.

At first he felt exultant: he had found out where the mysterious phrases came from; he had made an unexpected friend in Miss Oldman. She had let his words in. They had read together under the light of her lamp.

After a while, the exultation passed. Instead, a sweet melancholy grew in Gary like a sodden flower. His triumph, having produced the exultation, became now the very source of his sadness. There was no joy, really, in seeing a little more clearly, especially when it didn't make him more efficacious. Prof. Marshall would continue to block publication of the disputed manuscripts. He would die eventually and then, like the carcass of a watch-dog, all his fervour would be kicked aside and everyone would rush to get at what he had guarded.

Would they find Etta there? Would it even matter to them if they did or not? Would they take the trouble to bury what they unearthed? Gary was appalled to discover that custodial feelings had developed in himself. No, no: Etta had had enough protectors! What she needed now was for her words to be taken out and scattered, to fight the wind and the whimsy of the world as best they could.

And what of the page of cryptic references? Was he any closer to their interpretation or intention, simply because he knew where they came from? Something was apocryphal, that much was clear. But what was it? Looking over her life, he wondered whether it was the long rebellion or the final submission to conformity that was apocryphal. Was the life the apocryphon to the work or vice-versa? And what was the greater crime – that some of her work didn't get into the canon, or that some of it did?

The long line of the highway unrolled itself before him and the great lights that lit it bent over as if to sanction his passage. Gary felt as if he were being invited to drive forever, as if all destinations had unobtrusively been dispensed with and to move on and on and on was consummation enough.

Under the Dragon's Tail

My father almost got the part that went to William Holden. That's not just a rumour: it's been written about by people in the know. My father did such a good screen test that, although he was only twenty-six years old at the time and he hadn't even begun to make a name for himself, they took him seriously. I've also read that Billy Wilder was impressed with him at the time and wanted to give him a chance. But the studios always want the big names. That's how it is in Hollywood. Everyone knows that. Anyway, the upshot was that the part went to William Holden and my father had to wait another five years, doing bit parts, before he got his big break. Now, whenever I watch *Sunset Boulevard*, I think that it could so easily have been him in that role of the dead man in the swimming-pool who comes back to tell his story. He could have started his career in the same movie that revived the career of Gloria Swanson. Well, it was not to be. But later on he did get a chance to work with Billy Wilder. When he was interviewed by Dick Cavett, my father said that William Holden did a fine job. Besides, he said, he doesn't believe in regrets.

My father has been in Whodunits and Westerns and once he even played a bank clerk who bores his wife so much that she has an affair with another man. But he was hopelessly miscast in that role. It just wasn't believable. As Bette Davis said when she had to cheat on Joseph Cotten in *Beyond the Forest*, who would want to cheat on Joe Cotten? It's the same with my father. He simply cannot be boring, no matter how hard he tries, and especially not to women. His best roles have been ones in which they made use of his good looks. He can be suave and charming and sinister in a handsome sort of way. When he was younger, he was good at playing the type of man a father warns his daughter against. The daughter knows, in her secret heart, that her father is right. But she will never admit it and she goes off with the young man anyway and has a horrible life and grows old before her time. But she still keeps a photograph of him, taken when they went together to Bermuda or to Cannes, in the drawer of her bedside table. My father can do seductive evil any day. That's why he's so good in thrillers.

Although, as I said, he doesn't believe in regrets, I think that he has always been sorry that he didn't have an opportunity to work with Hitchcock. Can you imagine how good they would have been together? He almost got the part that went to Farley Granger in *Strangers on a Train*, but they said they wanted someone who was fresh-faced and innocent-looking. How short-sighted of them! My father can do fresh-faced and innocent, especially when it's the kind of innocence that quickly slips into depravity. Today you hardly hear of Farley Granger and my father is so well known. Well, that's how things turn out in that business.

There was an interview with my father last year in one of those film magazines that I subscribe to, and he said that Hollywood is a capricious place. It's a good word. He has what they call the gift of the gab. Capricious. Well, I think that makes it all the more remarkable that he's had such a successful and solid career: he's made more than fifty films and he hasn't slowed down. He's as busy as ever. They still want him even though he's over seventy years old. They call him a living legend. You might say that's what they call everyone who didn't end up like Elvis or Marilyn or James Dean or Jayne Mansfield or Sal Mineo or Carole Lombard. But I still think it's pretty good, especially for a boy who was born into a poor family in Johannesburg and who saw his first film at the Alhambra bioscope in Doornfontein.

There have been quite a number of South African actors who made it abroad. I have a special interest in them, because of my father. And I get irritated when people simply forget about the older actors. Young people today have no interest in the past. They know who Charlize Theron is, because she's in today's newspapers. At a push they might have heard of Alice Krige or Antony Sher or Janet Suzman. But if you mention Laurence Harvey to them, they just look blank. Laurence Harvey! My father and Laurence Harvey knew each other when they were children. And as for Moira Lister or Glynis Johns or Juliet Prowse or Sid James or Cecil Kellaway or Basil Rathbone, they haven't got a clue. 'Basil *who*?' they say. 'Who *are* these people?' It's a disgrace. Besides, it's unjust. I mean, what's the use of being famous if you get forgotten anyway after a while?

It's awful to be forgotten. I can't bear it when people are just pushed aside. It affects them terribly, especially those who once had the world at their feet. They can't get used to having had it all once, and now they've got nothing. I mean, look what happened to Gloria

Swanson in *Sunset Boulevard*. Is it any wonder she went off the rails? After such fame as she had, her obscurity was like a punishment.

I read that when Barbara Stanwyck was old and sick, no one came to see her. She said, 'Please don't let me die alone.' That was the heading of the article – 'Please Don't Let Me Die Alone: Legendary Actress Abandoned by Everyone'. Can you believe it? Barbara Stanwyck! The magazine that I read it in gave her address and asked readers to write to her, to let her know that we remembered her and we cared. So I did. I kept a copy of the letter I wrote:

> *Dear Miss Stanwyck,*
> *Your fans will never forget you. I live in South Africa and I've never even been to America, but you have enriched my life more than you can ever know. Who can forget the mother who sacrificed everything for her daughter in 'Stella Dallas'? Or the manipulative woman who had such power over Fred MacMurray in 'Double Indemnity'? Or your other great roles?*
> *You are not alone. God bless you.*
>
> *Your admiring fan,*
> *Ursula Meyer.*
>
> *P.S. I should like you to know that my father is one of your colleagues. I am proud to be the daughter of Bertram Lorentz.*

Not long after that, Barbara Stanwyck died. I don't know whether she ever received my letter, but I like to think that she did and that it brought her some comfort before she died.

I make a point of not forgetting people just because they aren't a part of my life at that very moment. It's easy for me to remember Dr

Gerber's birthday and his wedding anniversary, because I've worked for him for fifteen years and I see him every day, Monday to Friday; but I also remember the birthdays of people I haven't seen in years and years. For instance, the woman who was the Matron in the Home where my mother spent her last years. My mother died twelve years ago and the Matron retired to the coast not long after that. But every year I send her a birthday card (her birthday is in November), and, a few weeks later, I send her a Christmas card. I'll do that for as long as she lives. That's how it should be, but I know that everyone's not like me. Some people have got the loyalty of a flea.

Many people ask my father where he got his name from. Of course, if you know where he grew up, as I do, then you don't have to be told. He was born in Bertrams and the adjoining suburb was Lorentzville. He didn't think that Jack Miller sounded snazzy enough (although, come to think of it, Ann Miller had a similar sort of name, and it didn't do her any harm!). Anyway, he called himself Bertram Lorentz. I suppose he felt that if Archibald Leach could become Cary Grant, Reginald Truscott-Jones could become Ray Milland and Harry Skikne could become Laurence Harvey, then there was no reason why Jack Miller couldn't become Bertram Lorentz. It's not a bad name. It could have been worse: after all, he belongs to an industry that produced people with names like Rip Torn and Red Buttons! Anyway, I've noticed that his friends all call him Bertie. Last year the motion picture industry honoured him with a Lifetime Award at a special gala dinner (we saw it on TV), and, when they called on Shirley MacLaine to pay tribute to him, she said, 'Bertie Lorentz, you're one helluva guy!'

The strange thing is that I resemble my father quite strongly. The reason I say it's strange is because I'm no oil painting – not by a long shot. I never have been. But I have his eyes and lips, although I have my mother's round face. My father has classic good looks which have lasted well. His hair is silvery-grey now, but he still has his own teeth, his skin is good and he's not overweight. His is the kind of look that was popular in Hollywood at the time – you could see that same look in a number of other actors: Tyrone Power, Robert Taylor, Dana Andrews, John Payne, Fernando Lamas, Ricardo Montalban. It's gone out of fashion – now they want pretty boys like Rob Lowe. But in my father it's still acceptable, because he's an older actor now and middle-aged or elderly women are the only ones who are going to appreciate his looks nowadays.

Not surprisingly, he's had many relationships with women: in addition to his three marriages, there are rumours that he had affairs with most of his leading ladies. The ones that are mentioned most often are Gina Lollobrigida, Rita Moreno and Shelley Winters. But he will never talk about it. Although he often played the young man who loves-'em-and-leaves-'em, in real life he treats women with great respect. He even remained on good terms with his ex-wives. Two of them were at the gala dinner. In an interview with Barbara Walters, he said that he's disgusted by the modern tendency to sell the intimate details of one's life to the media. Nothing would persuade him to do that. He said he respects discretion and tact. He gave Jane Wyman as an example. She must have been offered millions to tell the story of her marriage to Ronald Reagan, but she kept a dignified silence.

The interesting thing about my father is that, despite the life that he has led and the parts he tended to play, he's a conservative man. He has been an outspoken member of the Republican Party ever since he became an American citizen. He appeared on platforms with his old friend Ronald Reagan and he knew President Ford and the first President Bush too. People always expect film stars to be left-wing, like

Jane Fonda or Vanessa Redgrave, but they forget how many of them have been staunch conservatives – Charlton Heston, for instance, or Bob Hope or Jimmy Stewart or Shirley Temple. My father is in good company. He's been criticised for the advertisements he's done on behalf of the National Rifle Association, but he says that all he is doing is defending the right of people to own arms and protect themselves. He doesn't even like hunting.

On the wall next to my desk at work I have photographs of all my favourite movie stars. There are more of my father than anyone else, but they're mixed in amongst the others so that they don't stand out in any way. Dr Gerber always teases me about my collection of photographs and about my love for the movies. Sometimes he tries to catch me out: he asks me who starred with so-and-so in such-and-such a film. I almost always know the answer. Or else he looks up something in a film reference book and then he comes to test me. 'Name the actress who was the sister of Gypsy Rose Lee,' he says.

'You'll have to do better than that,' I say. 'It's too easy.'

'So what's the answer?'

'June Havoc, of course.'

'All right, here's another one. Who was the first husband of Jessica Tandy – before she married Hume Cronyn?'

'You're not doing well today, Dr Gerber,' I say, rolling my eyes. 'These are as easy as pie.'

'So what's the answer?'

'Jack Hawkins, of course.'

'Ursula,' he says, 'you should enter a quiz show. You would win!'

'No,' I say. 'That's not my scene.'

'What a pity,' he says. 'I'd like to be able to boast about you.'

Dr Gerber is one of those caring general practitioners you seldom find these days. He still does home visits. And he never rushes his patients, no matter how many people there are in the waiting-room. I've been doing his accounts and paperwork for fifteen years and, in all this time, we've never had a cross word. He went regularly to the Home to see my mother throughout her long illness (my mother had Motor Neurone Disease – you know, like David Niven), and, when she died, Dr Gerber cancelled his appointments and he and his wife both came to the funeral. I will never forget that.

Last year my father came to South Africa to make a movie. During the apartheid years, he refused to work here. Although he's conservative when it comes to American politics, he has always been strongly opposed to the racial policies in this country. Shortly after he arrived, he was interviewed on television and he said he was proud to work in the country of his birth. The person who interviewed him seemed to know almost nothing about him or his career. I felt embarrassed about some of the things she was asking him. But my father answered all her questions courteously. He's not fazed by anything, you can see that. After so many years in the industry, he's a true professional. Our local actors and glitterati look like bumbling amateurs next to him. He is the real thing.

My father spoke about the movie he came to this country to make. He said it would be a joint American–South African production. Although the director and the main actors were from overseas, the smaller parts would be played by South Africans and many of the technicians and film crew would be South African. He and the director were anxious to develop the great talent that exists here and to give gifted young people some much-needed experience and exposure. 'Once the potential is there, all you need is a lucky break,' he said. 'I should know. I went to Hollywood as a brash young nonentity.

And I didn't become famous overnight. I struggled for five years. I cleaned cars and drove hearses and worked on a construction site. And then I had my lucky break.'

If the interviewer had been worth her salt, she would have asked him how he got his lucky break. It was the obvious question; I'm sure he was expecting it. But instead she asked him what the film he was working on would be called.

'*Under the Dragon's Tail*,' he replied.

'What a fascinating title,' she said. 'What does it mean?'

'It comes from Shakespeare,' he said. 'From *King Lear*. Edmund, the bastard son of the Duke of Gloucester, is talking about the circumstances of his birth. He says, "My father compounded with my mother under the dragon's tail." It's astrological – it refers to sin and wickedness.'

'Tell us a little about the film,' said the interviewer. You could see that Shakespeare made her nervous.

'It's based on a story that I came across a long time ago – before I left South Africa. It's a rich family saga, stretching from the years of the Anglo-Boer War until the end of the Second World War. It's got all the right ingredients: dark secrets, divided loyalties, sibling rivalries, bitter family feuds. Most of all, it's about land and the struggle for land – that is, after all, the story of this country. The main character is a wealthy landowner in what used to be the Northern Transvaal. He's a widower who has three children – in a way, it's *King Lear* all over again, except that it's very much a story of Africa. It also happens to be a true story. I always promised myself that I would do something with it, as soon as it became acceptable to work in South Africa again. It's taken a long time, but it's finally happening. Two writers – one of them an expatriate South African – took the story

I told them and turned it into an outstanding screenplay. The cast couldn't be better and we have one of my favourite directors. I'm co-producing the movie and acting in it. We're all set to go! My dream is finally coming true.'

'Where will the film be shot?'

'Mostly in the town of Haenertsburg and in the nearby Magoebaskloof mountains.'

The interviewer wished him well, but I hardly heard what she said. I paced up and down in my flat. Finally, I was able to work out a plan of action. The first thing was to ask Dr Gerber for leave. I knew that would not be a problem: I have oodles of leave due to me that I have never used, and Dr Gerber is always urging me to go on holiday. He must have been surprised that I wanted it immediately and that I didn't give him advance warning – I admit that was very uncharacteristic of me – but all he said was that he would arrange for a temp and that he hoped I had a good break.

Then I had my car serviced. The front tyres were a little worn, so I bought two new ones. I've had my car for eight years, but I almost never go on long trips, so it hasn't even done 50 000 kilometres. 'Where are you going, Miss Meyer?' the mechanic asked me.

'To the Northern Transvaal – I mean, to Limpopo Province. I forgot for a second that the name has changed.'

'Amazing how quickly everything is changing, isn't it? Well, I suppose there's no use trying to live in the past.'

'I have no intention of doing anything of the sort,' I said.

It was so long since I'd been to the North that I scarcely recognised the road. The last time I went there was with my mother, before she fell ill. I had no cause to go there without her. It was terribly hot. I stopped in Naboomspruit and then again in Potgietersrus (they both have new names too) to buy a cold drink. The cafe in Naboomspruit smelt of hot oil and chips. I bought a magazine and thumbed through it. There was an article about Michael Douglas in it. I think he's such an over-rated actor – you can't compare him to his father. And they made such a fuss about *Fatal Attraction*: in the meantime, there was a much better movie, years ago, on exactly the same subject – Clint Eastwood's *Play Misty for Me*. There's one more thing that's been forgotten. Honestly, it's like being surrounded by goldfish: they say a goldfish has such a short memory that by the time it gets to the other side of the bowl, it's already forgotten what it's just seen.

When I got to Polokwane (that's what Pietersburg is called now), I had some trouble finding the road to Tzaneen, but eventually I came right. I had forgotten how dramatically the landscape changes. Suddenly the yellow veld gives way to lush gorges and tropical vegetation. I didn't know which hotel the film crew was staying in, but a few discreet enquiries gave me the information I wanted. Then I even managed to get a room in the same hotel! I felt quite impressed with my efficiency.

As I went down to supper, I passed the bar of the hotel. I glanced in and got quite a shock. My father was sitting at a table near the door of the bar, talking to a group of young people. His back was turned to me, but he was so near that I could almost have touched him. He had a soft drink in his hand – he doesn't drink or smoke. He was telling a long story and the young people seemed to be engrossed in it. Well, so they might! Hearing that voice (people have compared his voice to Vincent Price's) made me feel quite emotional. I went to the dining-room and had my supper. I didn't have much of an appetite. I sat wondering what I should do next. Everything had gone so smoothly; I didn't want to make a mess of it now. How should I let my father know that I was here? In the end, I decided to write a letter and leave it for him at the front desk.

I sat up till all hours working on that letter. I rewrote it seven or eight times. I wanted it to be just right. I wished that I had my father's way with words, or even my mother's. My mother was a soft-spoken woman, but she chose her words very carefully and she was a wonderful story-teller. She made the past seem so vivid. I have never forgotten what she told me about her childhood on the farm, or the War years when she went to Johannesburg, or the years just after the War when she met my father. I scratched my head for a long time and cursed my limitations. What I settled on eventually didn't seem too bad:

> *My dear father,*
> *No doubt you will be astonished to receive this letter. Believe it or not, I am staying in the same hotel! I could have knocked on your door and said hello, but I thought I would write a letter and give you a chance to get used to the idea that I am here.*
>
> *I cannot tell you how excited I am that we will meet at last. I have dreamed of this moment ever since I discovered you were my father. I just know that we will get on well. I wonder if you ever received the letters I wrote to you? All I had was your agent's address, so perhaps they never got to you. Never mind, we will make up for lost time.*
>
> *In case you never did get those letters, I should explain that I am the daughter that was born to you and Mercia Meyer before you left South Africa. I am fifty-one years old and I live in Johannesburg. Not only am I your daughter, but I am also your biggest fan.*

I am in room 113. Please let me know when it will be convenient for us to meet. Perhaps in the evening, when you get off the set?

Looking forward to hearing from you,

Your affectionate daughter,
Ursula Meyer.

That night I could hardly sleep. I tried to watch TV, but there was nothing but junk: Sylvester Stallone and music videos. If I'd been at home, I could have watched *Sunset Boulevard* again, or another of my favourite movies – I have them all on tape. Instead I tossed and turned, imagining what the next day would bring. Would my father knock on the door of my room? Would he push a note under my door or leave one for me at the front desk, suggesting a time for us to get together? And when we did meet, how much we would have to speak about! Would he trust me enough to set aside his famous discretion and take me into his confidence? Would he tell me the truth about Gina Lollobrigida and Rita Moreno and Shelley Winters? What would he say when the time came to speak? And what would I say?

The next day turned out to be a terrible disappointment. Nothing happened. I waited in my room, but my father didn't appear. I asked the man at the front desk again and again if there was a message for me, but there was nothing. I hoped to see my father when I went down to supper, but there was no sign of him. I had a headache which was steadily getting worse. It seemed as if one of my migraines was advancing on me. Eventually I decided to go to bed. Perhaps he had had a very busy day on the set and would look for me the next day. As I walked through the foyer of the hotel towards my room, I suddenly saw him, talking to a group of people. It occurred to me that I had never seen him alone. He always seemed to be surrounded by an entourage. I heard them making plans to meet later in the bar and then he left the group and began walking towards me. My heart began to beat rapidly. He nodded at me and walked past. I turned around and called out to him: 'Excuse me! Mr Lorentz!'

'Yes?' He turned back and looked at me.

'Mr Lorentz, I'm Ursula Meyer. I wonder if you received my letter?'

'Did you write that letter?' he asked.

'Yes.'

'I refuse to discuss it with you now. I will write to you about it in the morning.' With that, he turned around and strode away. I couldn't believe my ears! I'd never heard that tone in his voice before. In the movies, if he has to be angry or unpleasant, his voice grows softer and he narrows his eyes. But here he was almost barking at me!

By the time I went to bed, I had a migraine. I have suffered from migraines most of my life. Each migraine is like a creature that settles on top of my head. It has a long tail with barbs in it, and it coils the tail around my head, very gently at first, and then tighter and tighter until the barbs bite into my head and I whimper with pain and beg for release. My mother used to bathe my forehead and rub my neck. She was the one who urged me to think of the migraine as a beast with a tail. 'Don't fight with the beast,' she would say. 'Make peace with it. Don't come between it and its anger. Make peace with it. Then it will release its grip.'

'I can't,' I would moan. 'I can't!' But sometimes it did work: I would try to welcome the thing that I loathed and the terrible pain, squeezing the sides of my head, would subside. That night, however, nothing helped, not even the pills which I kept swallowing. I longed to hear my mother's voice in the darkness, tranquil and soft, saying, 'Ursula, make your peace, make your peace'; but all I heard was laughter from the bar below and car doors slamming in the distance.

In the morning, the pain was gone but I felt woozy and my tongue was thick and furry in my mouth. I staggered to the door and, sure enough, there was a letter that had been pushed under it. The big, sharp letters seemed to jump at me as I read them:

> *Dear Ms Meyer,*
>
> *I must tell you that you are completely and utterly mistaken. I do not know how you came to form such a notion, but it could not be further from the truth. The relationship that you believe to exist between us has not the slightest basis in reality. I have never heard of Mercia Meyer. I have no daughter. We are nothing to each other.*
>
> *I am sorry that you have come so far in vain. I must ask you, however, not to approach me and to refrain from communicating with me in any way. Beyond that, it is not for me to tell you what you should or should not do. However, if you would allow me to offer some friendly advice, I would suggest that you return to Johannesburg immediately and put the entire episode out of your mind.*
>
> *Yours sincerely,*
> *Bertram Lorentz.*

I don't have the words to tell you how I felt when I read this letter. I simply could not believe what was before me. My own father was disowning me. He had written me a letter that was cold, cold, cold as ice. 'We are nothing to each other,' he had written. Nothing! Never had the word 'nothing' seemed so awful. Never had it seemed so empty. I sat on the bed, staring stupidly at the letter and reading it over and over again, torturing myself.

I managed to drag myself into the shower and then I felt a little better. I spent the rest of the day snoozing on my bed and recovering from the migraine. At dinner, I heard my father and his entourage making plans to go for a hike in the mountains near the hotel the next day. It was Sunday and they would not be working. My father, despite his age, is extremely fit. He has always been a great hiker. He loves the outdoors. Although he lives in California, he also owns a ranch in Montana and he goes there as often as he can. That night he seemed to be in a very good mood. I could see that he was enjoying the company of the young actors and actresses and film crew. He slapped the young man on his right on the back and put his arm around the young woman who sat to the left of him. The young people were tall and slim, tanned and self-confident. Their table was surrounded by laughter and my father sat smiling in the middle of it. All the light in the room seemed to be gathered around that group. I bolted my food and went to bed.

The next morning, I watched from the hotel foyer as the group set off on their hike and then I followed them, keeping far back. It was hot and muggy and the perspiration was soon pouring off me. A middle-aged couple caught up with me and kept me company. We spoke about the hotel, the food, the weather.

'Did you know they're shooting a movie here?' the husband asked me.

'Yes, I believe so,' I said.

'The film crew are staying in the hotel,' the wife said. 'Do you remember an actor called Bertram Lorentz? He was South African-born, but he became a big name overseas. He's starring in the movie.

I saw him in the hotel. He was very handsome when he was young. Mind you, he still looks good. He can put his shoes under my bed any day!'

'I remember him very well,' I said.

'I think it's going to rain,' the husband said.

'That's what you always say,' said his wife.

We were all three out of shape, so we stopped often to rest or to have something to drink. At about twelve o'clock we shared our sandwiches and biscuits. There was no sign of my father and his entourage. We were so high up that we couldn't even see the hotel any more. By the early afternoon, black clouds had begun to form above us. 'I told you so,' said the husband.

'I think we should turn back,' said the wife.

They tried to persuade me to return with them. I refused politely. They didn't want me to walk alone, but I assured them I would be fine. The pathway was clearly marked and there were people walking up and down all the time. They turned back and I went on alone. As the clouds grew thicker, a wind started up. The perspiration dried on me and I began to feel cold. My calves and thighs ached and my feet were killing me. The birds that had been chattering around us all the time fell silent and thunder rolled in the distance.

I came to a fork in the pathway. There was no way of knowing which way my father's group had gone. I would have to turn back. As I began the descent there was a crack of lightning, frighteningly near, and then the rain began to fall. There were some rocks near the pathway and I saw that one of them jutted out, making a sort of cave underneath. I ran towards it, scratching my face and arms against some thorns. Under the rock was a dark little cavity, musty and full of cobwebs, but at least it was dry. Outside the rain was coming down in sheets: I could scarcely see the path I'd been walking on. It was a cloudburst.

I wiped my bleeding arms and face with a tissue and then I burst into tears. I felt so low. I felt that this was the saddest moment of my life, sadder than when my mother was diagnosed with Motor Neurone Disease, sadder than the years of her tragic decline, sadder even than her death. I felt as if everything had been taken away from me. It was as if I had been stripped bare and my naked body was an affront to the eye – a hideous sight, especially to me. Here I was, crouching in a dirty cave, cold and bleeding, utterly alone, disowned by my own father: a woman of over fifty years old, yet as vulnerable as a child, suffering as a child no one wants must suffer. In my dejected state, I thought I would probably die in that dark place. I would die alone.

Eventually I stopped crying. There was more lightning and thunder and the storm grew fiercer by the minute. Although it frightened me, I also began to find it exhilarating. The more I watched it, the more my mournfulness faded away. Instead, I felt as if the storm was giving me some of its rage. All the anger I had felt since I received my father's letter suddenly washed over me. What a haughty letter it was, so stern and smug, so patronising! What right had he to write me such a letter? How could he just cast me aside? People all over the world loved him and he accepted their love, although they meant nothing to him. But he rejected the love and admiration of his own daughter.

I could feel another migraine coming on. My father's behaviour was – well, it was wicked! I never think of things as being wicked: it seems like an old-fashioned concept. But what he had done to me was truly wicked. And it was shabby! I could not get over the shabbiness of it. I thought of *Double Indemnity* and *Strangers on a Train* and

Shadow of a Doubt and *What Ever Happened to Baby Jane?* and *Hush … Hush, Sweet Charlotte*. There was wickedness in all of them. There was certainly evil. But it was stylish and clever. It was attractive. My father could give you that kind of evil without blinking an eye. He had given it to the world for years and years. Yet all he could give me was something shabby and mean.

In a way that I couldn't really understand, I felt as if his letter had made me feel ugly. It seemed like a physical insult. The handsome people of the world, all those whose lives were smooth, were in a conspiracy. The charmed circle had bolted its doors against me and left me out in the cold. I had come to see my father, proud of him and proud to be his daughter, but he had humiliated me and made me feel like a beggar. I longed for revenge. I didn't know how to take revenge, but I knew I couldn't allow myself to be treated in that way. I longed for the power to be wicked. I created a savage fantasy in which I saw him, broken and stricken with remorse, kneeling down before me and asking my forgiveness.

After a while the lightning and thunder seemed to let up, although it was raining as hard as ever. Suddenly I heard a noise outside the cave. When I stuck my head out, I saw something very strange: a misshapen giant, lurching about in the streaming rain and overturning stones as it walked, was descending the mountain. When it came closer, I saw it wasn't a giant after all, but a man carrying another one on his back. I called out loudly and they stopped and peered at me. Then they came towards me. It was one of the young men from the film crew and the man he was carrying on his back was my father.

'He's sprained his ankle very badly,' the young man shouted. He was an American. 'The others went on ahead and I was helping him down. Then we got caught in this storm.'

My father's face was screwed up with pain. He didn't seem to see me.

'Is it dry in there?' asked the young man.

'Yes,' I said. 'Do you want to come inside?'

'I may as well go down and get help. I couldn't possibly be any wetter than I am. But it would be great if I could leave him here. He's terribly heavy.' He helped my father into the cave. 'Bertie, I'm going to get help,' he said. 'Just wait here with this lady.' Then he disappeared into the rain.

My father groaned and rubbed his swollen ankle. He was shivering and his lips were blue. I couldn't believe how old and frail he seemed suddenly: the silver-haired man who carried his years with such ease and authority was gone. I had a light jersey that I had tied around my waist as I walked and then put on when it grew cold. It was damp, but it had dried out a little while I had been in the cave. Anyway, it was better than nothing. I took it off and put it around his trembling shoulders. He turned and looked at me for the first time. He didn't seem to know me at first, but then I could see the recognition grow in his eyes.

'Oh, it's you,' he said. 'Miss Meyer. I thought you'd gone back home.'

'No,' I said. 'I'm still here.'

'Following me, no doubt?'

'I can walk where I like,' I said. 'You don't own the mountain.'

He turned away and rubbed his ankle again. I looked at his hands. I've always been fascinated by people's hands. And I've always been proud of my own hands. Even though, as I've said, I'm no oil painting, I know that I have shapely hands. And I saw now where I got them from. My father's hands were beautiful. The fingers were just right:

not too long or too stubby, no horrible tufts of hair growing out of the knuckles. Angry as I was, his hands made me feel tender towards him.

'Is there anything I can do?' I asked. 'I can see you're in great pain.'

'I'll be all right,' he said. 'I get carried away and overdo things. I have to confess that I'm not a youngster any more.'

I rummaged in my rucksack and found a slab of chocolate and a fruit juice. I gave them to him. 'Thank you,' he said. 'You're very kind.'

We sat quietly. Although we did not speak, I felt that he was watching me. It made me feel uncomfortable. Eventually he said, 'What gave you the idea that you're my daughter? How did such a thing ever get into your head?'

'It's in my head because it's the truth,' I said. 'And whether you accept it or not, it will remain the truth.'

'But what made you *believe* such a thing?'

'I know it's the truth because my mother told me so. I don't know how you can deny that you knew her!'

'What did you say her name was?'

'Mercia Meyer.'

'It doesn't ring a bell. I'm sure I never met anyone by that name. I have a very good memory for names and faces.'

'I can prove that you knew her!'

'How?'

'Very easily. You know the story that you're filming right now – the widower from the Northern Transvaal and his three children? Well, that's my mother's story. That man was my grandfather and my mother was his youngest child. She grew up in this area. She told me the story of her family, just as she must have told it to you. Where else could you have heard it?'

'I heard it from a young man who came from this part of the world. He was also an aspiring actor. We met just after the War. He was killed in a diving accident not long afterwards.'

'Nonsense!' I was so angry. The migraine slid a little closer. 'You met my mother when you were working in a travelling theatre group after the War. You went from town to town, right across the platteland, putting on plays in town halls. I suppose you're going to deny that too?'

'Of course not. Why should I? I did that for two years. We put on mostly Afrikaans plays. My Afrikaans wasn't very good, but I worked at it. I gained a lot of experience. When the two years were up, I took the money that I'd earned, went down to Cape Town and boarded a ship. It was going to Southampton. From there, I crossed the Atlantic. The rest, as they say, is history.'

'My mother was also a member of that group,' I said. 'She did the costumes and she worked on the sets. She was a very artistic young woman. I know exactly where you went: you started off in Potchefstroom and Klerksdorp. From there you went to Wolmaransstad. I even know where I was conceived.'

'Ursula,' he said. 'May I call you Ursula? I'm telling you that I did not know her. Believe me, I would remember. Perhaps it was another theatre group? You should ask her ...'

'She's dead,' I interrupted him. 'She died twelve years ago. Of Motor Neurone Disease – you know, like David Niven.'

'I'm very sorry,' he said. 'It's a terrible illness. I know how David suffered.'

Tears came into my eyes and I blinked them away impatiently. 'If I have to choose between her version and yours, I prefer to believe what she told me,' I said. 'I never knew her to tell a lie.'

He moved closer to me. 'What do you want from me?' he asked. 'If you've got some crazy idea of blackmailing me, I can tell you that you'll get nowhere.'

'It's not about money,' I said.

'That's what they all say.'

'All I want is recognition. That's all I've ever wanted. I know that people in your circles suffer all the time from paternity suits and things like that and, for the most part, I feel sorry for them. I really do. I have no desire to harm your reputation – or, at least, that was how I felt when I came here. Now I'm angry and bitter, so there's no knowing what I'll do. As I said in my letter, I'm your biggest fan. But I want what is due to me.'

'Even if it's not due to you? Even if you're living someone else's lie? Or her delusion?'

'That's not possible,' I said. Then we sat silently again. We were stuck. I wondered if there was some way to force him to take a blood test. I didn't want to waste money on lawyers, but perhaps I could ask Dr Gerber to recommend one when I got back to Johannesburg?

'Aren't you cold?' my father asked. 'You should take your sweater back.'

'Keep it,' I said sourly. 'I'll survive.'

He got to his feet and hobbled to the front of the cave. 'I'm going outside,' he said. 'I have to relieve myself. You know what old men's bladders are like.'

I called him back. 'You can do it here,' I said. 'I don't mind. Come out of the storm.'

I turned my back while he urinated. 'I wonder why they haven't come to look for us yet?' I asked.

'They must be waiting for the rain to stop. But it shows no sign of doing so. And it's going to start getting dark soon.'

'How's the ankle?'

'Very sore. I hope it's not broken. Thank you for your concern.'

He sat down opposite me and groaned again. 'I'm not very good company, I know,' he said. 'I'm sorry. You must bear with me.'

'It's all right,' I muttered. 'I'm no Jack Benny myself.'

'I knew Jack Benny,' he said. 'I knew him well.'

'Really?' I couldn't hide my interest. He told me about Jack Benny. Somehow, from that, we got to speaking about George Burns and Martha Raye. Without realising it at first, I witnessed an astonishing transformation. My father became charming. As we sat trapped in that dismal cave as if in a cage, I saw for myself what his charm was, what it could do, how irresistible it was. He asked me about myself and he seemed truly interested in what I had to say. He listened carefully and he seemed to affirm my little world without gushing.

Then he spoke about himself. He told me the most wonderful stories and anecdotes. I had never heard them before. I forgot about everything except what he was telling me. The migraine that had been threatening me turned tail and fled. As it grew darker, I couldn't distinguish my father's features any more. All I could see was the shape of his head. His rich voice filled the cave. I got all the latest Hollywood gossip – who's in, who's out. I can tell you that what you read in the magazines is nothing compared to what you get from the horse's mouth. I heard about the early years when he first got to Hollywood, about the famous people he worked with and what they were really like. I heard what Bogart said to him and why Joan Crawford hated him and why Douglas Fairbanks Jr. once said, 'I owe you one, Bertie!', and what it's like to dine in the White House with Ron and Nancy.

I didn't even notice that the rain had stopped. We heard people calling in the distance. We were being rescued. 'Give me your hand,' I said. I helped him out of the cave. It was dark outside.

I was sorry to have our conversation interrupted. There was so much more that I wanted to know. I had a thousand questions that I wanted to put to him. I did manage, however, to ask him about Gina Lollobrigida and Rita Moreno and Shelley Winters. He said it was two-thirds true: he did have a relationship with two of them. But he definitely did not become romantically involved with one of the three. That was just a false rumour. In that industry, where there's so much back-biting and people prey on each other all the time, they have to contend with false rumours. And my father told me – he actually *told* me – which two it was that he had a relationship with. But it was told to me in confidence and so I cannot say.

Indian Summer

Because it was the middle of April, people called it autumn. But the nights were still warm and showers of rain fell every few days. The first camellias and the last roses were flowering at the same time.

These were slow, discreet days, the gift of a lingering season.

Outside the house was a sign which said that it had been sold and congratulated the estate agent. Inside Doris and Laura were wrapping ornaments and crockery in newspaper and putting them in cardboard boxes. As they sealed each box, Laura numbered it and made a note of its contents in a small notebook. Monty and the gardener were cleaning out the garage and the garden shed. The women could hear their voices and the scraping sounds of objects being dragged across a cement floor.

They took a tea-break. Monty came in with blackened hands and cobwebs in his hair. He washed his hands, but, as he wasn't aware of the cobwebs, he did nothing about them. They sat outside, enjoying the warmth of the sun.

Monty was always a demonstrative man and now he touched Laura often, patting her on the head or the shoulder. Once she took his hand, so big and rough, in her own and smiled at him. Doris, noticing this, sighed. 'If you don't come and visit us in America, Laura,' she said, 'I don't know what we'll do.'

'Of course I will,' said Laura.

But she had her doubts.

Her continued friendship with Doris and Monty, even after her divorce from their son, was more than unusual: it was a miracle; a freak of love. Laura had been amazed to find, after she and Howard were divorced, that nothing altered in his parents' affection for her. These two conventional people stepped outside their conventionality and made a friend of an ex-daughter-in-law. And so she had been able to harvest their loyalty to her when she needed it most.

But could even so rare an attachment survive a separation as vast as the one that now loomed?

She had thought often of losing them, but never imagined that it would be to anything other than death. They would die in Johannesburg, she had presumed; they would be buried in West Park Cemetery. It had never crossed her mind that they might leave the country. Many people were emigrating, but they were, for the most part, young professional people – like Howard. The older generation tended to stay behind, poring over photographs, making occasional visits to children and grandchildren in Atlanta, Irvine, London, Toronto, Sydney.

And, indeed, Monty and Doris had seemed resigned to their elderly forlornness. But Howard came out to South Africa determined to convince them to leave. He had met an American woman, he told them; he was going to marry her; her name was Candy; they planned to start a family very soon. Surely they wished to know their grandchildren, to watch them growing up?

He dealt with their misgivings one by one. He would buy them an apartment very near his own. It would have central heating and air-conditioning. He would put them on his medical aid and take out extra medical insurance. And, after all, he remonstrated, what was there here for them? They were both retired and their already-depleted circle of friends was rapidly diminishing further.

Yes, there was Laura; he was not underestimating what Laura meant in their lives. He could never be sufficiently grateful to her for what she did for them. But she had her own life to lead. Did that not occur to them? Perhaps she too would remarry one day; perhaps she too would move away. He was their son, their only child; he was the person they should be relying on in their old age, not Laura.

It was not his logic or his perseverance or his enthusiasm that did it in the end, Laura believed. It was his charm, which had served him well for so long. No one knew better than she the power of that charm. It was inseparable from his beauty, from the self-assurance which his beauty gave him. Monty and Doris had never had physical beauty of their own; they had been drawn to each other initially because they were reassured by each other's plainness – Doris had confessed as much to Laura. Yet they had produced a child of uncommon beauty. The gratification which this provoked in them never abated, so that they were proud, absurdly proud, to think that such beauty had hidden within them, unknown to them. And when Howard used that power, they couldn't resist it, for he was using what they were themselves secretly so enamoured of; he was turning upon them the force of their own bountiful surprise.

So they gave in.

And Laura could not blame them, for in their eyes his charm had never been contaminated as it had in hers; his beauty had never been defiled.

But now, as she sat with them, something bitter and hard came into her heart. It was self-recrimination. In saying nothing, in tacitly approving of the emigration, she knew that she had let them down. She had made all the gestures of friendship: she had helped them to pack up, she would take them to the airport, she would have power of attorney over their bank accounts; but for all that, she had let them down.

She had been a deficient friend.

A true friend would have expressed her misgivings. A true friend would have told them that she did not trust Howard; did not trust him to care for them in that strange place; did not trust him at all.

Laura, were she such a friend, would have told Doris and Monty that, no matter how much they loved him – and there was no end to their love for their son – it was she, not they, who *knew* him.

But she had not known how to say these words. There was no tradition of blunt talk in their friendship, which, because of the unusual circumstances in which its continuation had been secured, was woven out of a tact as fine as gossamer.

The very restraint they had nurtured had made possible her great crime of omission. She was culpable because she could not bear to cloud the Indian summer of their wondrously sustained friendship.

A hoopoe landed on the grass in front of them. 'I wonder,' said Doris, 'whether I shall grow to love the birds in America as I do here?' No one replied. 'And do you know,' she went on, 'whether they have crickets there? I love the sound of crickets.'

They sat silently in the lap of a warm, desultory breeze.

Friendly Fire

There was a time when loyalty gave the answer.

Linda kept close to her always the memory of that autumn afternoon. She was a child, a diffident and doubting child; but on that day a solemn assurance was handed to her. It told her that she wouldn't have to do battle alone. Through all the years that lay ahead, it promised her, through those capricious years, a thread of staunchness would run.

It was a Sunday afternoon in April when she was ten years old and Pam was almost twelve. Linda was alternately obsequious and resentful as scorned younger sisters are, Pam as disdainful as older sisters who aspire to be sophisticated need to be. They had little to do with each other.

They were visiting the Moller twins, Maureen and Gillian, on their farm. Pam and Linda's parents knew the twins' mother and father slightly and had been invited for the first time for afternoon tea. To the adults it was nothing more than a routine visit. But to Pam and

Linda it was momentous. At school Maureen and Gillian were by far the most popular girls. They were lithe, blond and sporty and had already turned twelve. They were known simply as 'the twins'. They had created and then placed themselves at the centre of a charmed circle into which only selected girls were allowed. Pam wasn't one of them. They scarcely acknowledged her presence and were unlikely even to have noticed that she had a younger sister. Pam longed to be chosen by them. Linda cherished no such hope, for she knew it lay beyond the bounds of possibility; but she would at least be able to tell the girls of her own age that she 'had been invited with her sister to the twins' farm', and that would give her a small stake in the charmed circle.

They felt anxious as they arrived at the farm, wondering if they would be snubbed here too as Pam had been at school, but they found the twins to be surprisingly friendly and welcoming. Maureen and Gillian pretended to both sets of parents that they and Pam were friends at school and paid lip-service to a history which had never existed. 'Do you remember when Vollie dropped his glasses and stood on them?' Maureen said, turning to Pam. Vollie was Mr Volschenk, the elderly science teacher.

'Yes,' said Pam. 'And then he couldn't see a thing!'

'Blind as a bat,' said Gillian.

In fact, Pam had never witnessed this event. She wasn't in the twins' class that term. But nothing would make her admit that. Through circumstances created by her parents, she had a chance of sneaking by another route into the charmed circle; and she intended to grasp the opportunity as firmly as possible.

The unwonted friendliness of the twins was not the only surprise of the afternoon. The other was the drabness of the farm. The confidence and superiority exuded by Maureen and Gillian had implied a life Pam and Linda read about in books about British children: rolling paddocks, glossy horses, gymkhanas, mounds of sweet-smelling hay. But the Moller farm smelled of dung and mouldy leaves. There were no horses to be seen, only pigs and chickens. The farmhouse was small and the walls needed a fresh coat of paint. The twins seemed reluctant to show them their bedrooms and, when they finally did, Pam and Linda saw that it was because there was only one small bedroom, which they shared. And the wallpaper in their bedroom was embarrassingly babyish: bunny rabbits, pink and yellow, ascended and descended.

The Moller parents were also a surprise. The twins, despite their surname, had passed themselves off as English in every way. They led and encouraged the anti-Afrikaner snobbery which was rife at the school, even though the English-speaking children were in the minority. Their mother, who was pale and small, already shorter than her daughters, was indeed English speaking. But the father spoke with what was unmistakably a gruff Afrikaans accent.

Pam saw quickly that there were things the twins would not want known at school; and that made her all the more hopeful that she might be able to creep into their favour. She had witnessed aspects of the girls' lives which she could choose either to reveal or conceal. And that gave her power.

She would, of course, conceal what she had found, for what she sought was not the humiliation of the twins, but their public embrace of her.

The afternoon promised to be successful beyond her greatest hopes.

'Let's go outside,' Gillian said. 'We want to show you the barn.'

'Are there snakes there?' asked Linda.

'Oh, yes,' said Maureen, 'but don't worry about them. They're much more scared of you than you are of them.'

Linda wasn't reassured by this, but she accompanied them anyway.

What the sisters called the barn was a dank building which smelled of sacks and straw. The twins held the wooden door open for Pam and Linda and, once they were all inside, closed it behind them. The only light came through a single grimy window. They could hear scratching noises.

'What's that?' asked Linda.

'Probably rats,' said Maureen. 'They're *huge*.' She spread her arms as if making a benediction.

'They can't be *that* big,' said Pam.

'Wait and see,' responded Gillian. The girls' voices were muffled in the gloom and near-silence of the barn.

Linda wished she could go outside and leave the others to play their games, but she couldn't risk it: they would call her a sissy and she would jeopardise the burgeoning new friendship. Pam would never forgive her.

'Look what I found.' Gillian thrust something inside her hand. She closed her fingers around it nervously. It was round and smooth.

'What is it?' She unclasped her fingers.

'It's an egg.'

'Oh.' An egg didn't seem very remarkable. She wasn't sure how she was supposed to respond.

'Smell it,' said Maureen. 'And then shake it.'

She held it to her nose. 'Yuk,' she said. It smelled awful. And when she shook it, liquid sloshed around inside. 'Why does it smell like that?'

'Because it's a rotten egg. And that's why it makes that sound when you shake it.' Maureen took it from her and passed it on to Pam, who sniffed and shook the egg dutifully, and then handed it to Gillian.

'Let's play hide-and-seek,' suggested Maureen, turning round and flinging the barn door open.

They all agreed that this was a good idea. Linda was relieved that they were not going to stay in the barn any longer; but, to her dismay – without understanding why or how – she found that she was 'on'. She had to wait alone inside the barn and count to a hundred, and then go and look for the others.

She counted slowly, calling out the numbers softly under her breath. When she finished, she stood quite still. The scratching sounds – whatever they were – had stopped. Through the open door came long spears of rusty afternoon light. The barn, that had seemed so threatening to her, suddenly seemed peaceful. She relished the silence. She wished she could stay there until the game was finished. She was convinced that she wouldn't be able to find any of them – after all, who knew the farm and its many hiding-places better than the twins did? And they would help Pam to find a good hiding-place too. But she had to try. She owed it to herself. And to Pam.

She waited a few more seconds and then strode through the door. '*Coming – ready or not!*' she called out, as loudly as she could.

Not surprisingly, there was no sign of any of them. She wandered around, peering half-heartedly under bushes and behind the parked cars. She even looked in the pigsty. But the girls were nowhere to be found. 'I give up,' she shouted, but no one responded. She toyed with the idea of going back into the farmhouse and sitting with the adults, but she sensed that that wouldn't be a good idea. She searched on.

There was a windmill, a reservoir and cluster of willows quite a distance from the farmhouse and the outbuildings. Could they be hiding that far away? It seemed unlikely, but she walked slowly towards the trees. Then she paused. It was beginning to grow dark as the afternoon light receded. A cold wind had arisen. Beyond the willows lay the stubble of a reaped mealie field. Her throat was dry and she could hear her own breath. She reached the trees and stood there, her misgivings tugging at her. The windmill creaked and spat, creaked and spat.

No, no, she told herself – this was much too far from the homestead. They couldn't possibly be here. They were probably in the twins' bedroom, drinking Fanta and eating biscuits and laughing at her. She was about to turn back.

Then two things happened. The first was that she saw Pam, imperfectly hidden behind a discarded tractor tyre which lay next to the windmill. 'I can see you!' she shouted, filled with relief, beginning to run to her sister. 'Come *out*, Pam. I can see you.'

The second was that, as she moved towards her sister, she felt something land on her head. She stood there, puzzled, wondering what could have fallen on her. And what smelled so bad?

She looked around her; and then she looked up. And then she saw everything. And understood everything. There was a crude treehouse in one of the willows. The twins were both up there. They had waited there while Pam hid behind the tyre. And, as Linda passed beneath them, they had dropped the rotten egg – the same one they had shown her earlier – onto her head.

It was a perfectly executed plan; an immaculate treachery.

The liquid began to trickle down the back of Linda's head and onto her neck. She was too shocked to move; too shocked even to cry. The twins clambered down and stood at the base of the willow tree.

'Don't be upset,' said Gillian. 'It was just a joke.'

'We'll clean you up,' said Maureen.

Linda said nothing. She knew it was not a joke. And she knew that they would not be able to clean her or remove the smell – not ever.

'Our parents don't have to know,' said Maureen. She looked not at Linda, but at Pam. 'They don't have to know,' she repeated. 'It will be our secret. Won't it, Pam?'

'Our secret forever,' said Gillian.

There was silence. No one moved. The sun was setting and the wind picked up strength. Pam stood stiffly with her back to the reservoir. Linda shivered in the clearing. The twins, clearly anxious now about the consequences of what they had done, had not left their position at the foot of the tree.

Linda knew all too well what they were offering Pam: help us cover this up, they were saying; persuade your brat of a kid sister not to split on us, and we'll guarantee you your place with us at school. You will have made it. You'll be *in*.

Linda knew they would prevail. What they were extending could not be declined. In the silkiness of their unassailable popularity lay an appeal that Pam would not be able to resist. And what did she, Linda, have to offer instead? Nothing. Who would choose an encumbrance, a stinking little sister, over these envied twins? She lowered her head and waited for the inevitable.

When she looked up, Pam was standing in front of her. 'I didn't know what they were going to do,' she said. 'They told me to hide behind the tyre and they said they would hide in the tree-house. I didn't know anything about the egg.'

'Oh,' said Linda. 'Well, that's …'

'No, really. You have to believe me. I knew nothing about the egg. I promise you.'

'I believe you,' said Linda. 'I do.'

'Good. Now let's go and get you cleaned up.'

It was only when she had taken Linda's hand in hers and they were walking together away from the twins; only when Pam called out – without turning her head – and she heard the scorn in her sister's voice, only then did Linda begin to understand. 'What idiots you are! You two need to grow up,' shouted Pam. They walked on.

Linda at last grasped the full implications of what had happened.

Her sister had chosen her.

It was unbelievable.

They held hands until they reached the farmhouse. 'Shoo, it really does stink,' said Pam. 'I don't know how we're going to get you cleaned up. Your clothes will have to be washed.'

'I don't know either,' said Linda. But she didn't care. It didn't matter to her in the least whether they got her clean or not. All she could think of was the act of loyalty that she had witnessed; the gift of loyalty that she had received. It was huge: bigger than her; bigger than Pam. It was the greatest thing she'd ever known. It shone in the gathering darkness and transformed every corner of the sad little farm. It took every part of that late autumn afternoon, turned it round and gave it to her – to keep, to make her own. She became the conqueror where before she had been the one doomed to be vanquished.

'This will never, ever leave me,' she said solemnly to herself.

The twins never spoke to Pam or Linda again. And their parents had no more contact with the Mollers. They had remonstrated that afternoon with Mr Moller for punishing his daughters so severely – he didn't even wait for his visitors to leave before he beat the twins with a thick plank. In a cold voice, he told them that he didn't need anyone to tell him how to bring up his daughters. After that, no further invitations to visit the farm were extended.

For reasons that were not clear, the twins' popularity at school began to wane after the egg incident, even though neither Pam nor Linda told anybody about it. The charmed circle to which Pam had longed so fervently to be admitted ceased to exist.

Years later, Linda met a woman who had been at school with her and, in the way that old acquaintances from school do, they asked the expected questions: 'Do you remember so-and-so?' 'I wondered what ever happened to so-and-so?'

Then, for the first time, Linda heard what had happened to the twins. Maureen had died of breast cancer before her thirty-seventh birthday. Gillian had married young and had emigrated not long after her marriage to the US. She was living in Cleveland, said the acquaintance. Or was it Pittsburgh? Well, some place like that.

'My goodness,' said Linda. 'Is that really what happened to them? I can't believe it.' She couldn't reconcile any of this information with what she remembered of those cruel, beautiful girls. What she was being told was neither appropriate nor inappropriate; it was just *wrong*. The path they bestrode should have led to something consistent with their tawny hauteur – not to dying young or living in a place which was just a name to most of those who had once known them. It was all wrong. She shook her head in bafflement.

'And what about your sister?' asked the acquaintance. 'What was her name again?'

'Pam.'

'Oh, that's right. Pam. I remember now. She was a few years older than us. What's happened to her?'

'Oh, she's fine,' said Linda. 'She's very well.'

It was strange to consider that she had no idea whether she was uttering a lie or the truth. Pam could be fine and well; or she could be neither.

'She lives in Cape Town,' she added.

'And you? In Joburg?'

'Yes.'

'But you get together often?'

'Oh, yes.'

'Will you give her my regards?'

'Certainly,' said Linda.

She was not going to tell this woman – a stranger, despite their shared past – that she no longer spoke to her sister.

Pam was constantly in her thoughts, but she always appeared there unbidden. Linda didn't want to think of her, but she couldn't help it. And it was not one Pam who came there, but many: a child, a teenager, a young woman, getting married, becoming a doctor, getting divorced, moving to Cape Town. These faces merged, separated, became pallid and then grew vivid in a phantasmagoria of familiarity and strangeness. There would be long periods when her sister's ghostly presence seemed almost to recede, becoming nothing more than a barely audible call, the softest of supplications. 'She is dead to me now,' Linda had said when she discovered what had happened; and at such times it seemed to her as if her sister were indeed about to die out of her life; that the whisper would grow so faint that it would never be heard again. And then it would change: the wraithlike Pam would vanish, and she would re-appear as a strident, grating voice, penetrating Linda's dreams with hot denunciations – which was odd, for she, Linda, was the wronged one, the victim. Of what, then, was she being accused?

It was a Saturday afternoon and she lay on the couch in the living-room. Someone had switched the TV on. She found it intrusive, but couldn't bring herself to get up and put it off. She could hear it was CNN, with news from around the world:

> *earthquake off the coast of Indonesia, 6.7 on the Richter Scale*
> *suicide bombing in Pakistan, 22 dead*
> *four American soldiers die in Afghanistan; deaths attributed to friendly fire*

She dozed off and when she woke up again, she heard the same news items being repeated, in the same order:

> *earthquake off the coast of Indonesia, 6.7 on the Richter Scale*
> *suicide bombing in Pakistan, 22 dead*
> *four American soldiers die in Afghanistan; deaths attributed to friendly fire*

Why, she wondered, as she lay there, reluctant to dispel the lingering sweetness of the nap from which she had awoken, did they repeat the same news over and over again? Was nothing else happening in the world?

Then they interviewed a soldier who had been injured in the 'friendly fire' incident. He was not sure exactly what had happened. 'Last thing I remember,' he said, 'was an explosion to the right of us. And then another one.' He wiped his eyes. 'This will never, ever leave me,' he said.

There was something in what he said that set up an echo. *This will never, ever leave me* – spoken in an American accent – where had she heard that before? It seemed to lie close, yet she couldn't grasp it. Her drowsy mind reached out, almost seized it, but it scuttled away.

She gave up and thought instead about 'friendly fire'. What a strange concept it was. How extraordinary to expire in the cleft of a paradox! Once you were dead, you were dead – it would be of little consequence to you whether your death had been caused by hostile or friendly weaponry. But it would be of great significance to everyone else: the soldiers who had mistakenly killed their comrades; and, above all, the families of the dead soldiers. How must they feel? Was it better or worse to know that your loved one had been killed inadvertently? Wouldn't it be easier to accept a death caused by the enemy?

Yes, she decided. For her, if she were one of the bereaved, it would be easier. The avowed enemy was, if nothing else, avowed. You knew what to expect. But the injury from within: *that* was entirely another matter.

Eventually she got up, switched off the TV and washed her face. When Jon came home from his weekly golf game, she was in the kitchen, preparing dinner. He kissed her.

'Smells good,' he said. 'I'm famished.'

The worst day of Linda's life had begun uneventfully. Jon had flown to Singapore the previous evening. After dropping the children off at school, she went to work at the nursery and garden furniture shop which she co-owned with Delia, her best friend. They were busy all morning and, although she heard her cellphone ring, she didn't get to it in time to answer. When she glanced at it later, she saw that there was a missed call from Pam. She sent her a quick text message: *sorry i missed yr call hectic here call u later luv L.*

She was serving a customer when she heard a beep and, glancing down, saw her cellphone shudder as a message came through. 'How many bags of potting-soil?' she asked, reaching down to read the message.

She did not hear the customer's reply. Instead she stood still, shaking her head in puzzlement. The message must have been intended for someone else. It couldn't possibly be for her. Who would send her such a message? Who would make up such dreadful, preposterous lies?

'I said *six* bags.' The customer's voice rose in irritation.

'Andrew,' she called out, 'please bring six bags of potting-soil for the lady. No, we're not out of stock. They delivered more this morning.'

When the customer had left, she read the message again.

yr husbands having an affair

She scrolled down.

with yr sister

She thought when she was young that she liked deft, dark men with very white teeth and cryptic hands, but she changed her mind when she met Jon. He was blond and stooped a little as he walked. His hair was already thinning in his early twenties. He was a pilot, but he looked as if he should be a farmer or a game-ranger. His hands were warm (even on the coldest days) and broad. They were incapable of secrets – or so she thought.

As the years passed, many of her friends' marriages collapsed. Pam, too, got divorced. Other marriages ran into difficulties or limped along. Delia remained single and went from one lover to another. Linda thought with relief of her own marriage and of the blessings of constancy.

She never discovered who had sent her the anonymous sms. She mentioned it to Jon when he got back from Singapore, expecting him to scoff and laugh it off. And if he had done so, if he had told her it was the most ridiculous nonsense he had ever heard, she would have left it at that, for she truly suspected nothing. Jon's work took him frequently to Cape Town. He almost always saw Pam when he was there; sometimes he even stayed over at her home. He brought gifts from her for Linda and the kids and bore gifts from them to Pam. It was not a situation conducive to the spawning of secrets.

But Jon, to her astonishment, crumpled and confessed at once. He berated himself and begged her to forgive him. He even wept.

'With my *sister*!' It was grotesque. It was incestuous – not literally, perhaps, but it felt like incest. Such things did not happen to people like her. People who had affairs with their sister-in-law or brother-in-law were troglodytes, still casting off bits of primeval slime while they hurled abuse at each other on American talk shows.

'I know. I know.'

'You had … you and my sister!'

Jon went to the bathroom and returned with a tissue, into which he blew his nose. 'I don't know what to say to you, Linda. I'm so sorry. All I can say is that it's over. I promise you. Totally over.'

He kept insisting that they hadn't intended it to happen, that they knew it was terribly wrong and had tried to stop themselves. But she could scarcely pay attention to what he was telling her, for she was still in profound shock, struggling to comprehend the fact of a double betrayal.

As the days passed, all that was clear to her befuddled brain was that her husband and her sister had both broken something precious. They were equally responsible for the damage they had wrought. But what Jon had broken was not the same as what Pam had broken.

In the aftermath of the double deceit, Linda found herself under pressure to explain her decisions. People seemed to feel that they had the right to expect her to justify her choices to them.

Even Delia challenged her. 'Just tell me one thing,' she said. 'Why is what *she* did worse than what *he* did?'

There were no customers in the nursery and they were taking a tea break.

'I never said it was.' Linda sipped her tea.

'But then why can he be forgiven and she can't?'

'I don't know that he *has* been forgiven. Not yet, anyway.' She looked up. 'Have those African Violets been watered?'

'Yes. I watered them myself.' Delia poured herself another cup. She sat hunched forward, peering expectantly at Linda. She had a round, glistening face and short-cropped grey hair. 'Don't change the subject.'

'I'm not.'

'Then explain it to me. You must have forgiven Jon – you're still married to him, aren't you?'

'Well, we're working on our marriage. We're trying to save it. It's not clear yet whether we'll succeed.'

'But you've given him another chance.'

'Yes.'

'And yet you don't talk to Pam.'

'Correct. She is dead to me now.'

'But they both did the same thing – they hurt you in the same way. Why treat them differently?'

'To me it *is* different.'

'Is it that he's contrite and she's not?'

'No, not at all. If anything, she's more contrite. I think she truly regrets it. She's tried to apologise to me over and over again.'

'Then I return to my question. Why can he be forgiven and she can't? Why is what she did worse than what he did?'

Linda put down her cup and stood up. She walked to the door of their little office and looked out. It was a late summer afternoon. A bank of dark clouds was building up in the west. 'I think there's another thunderstorm on the way,' she said.

'Probably,' said Delia, also standing up. She walked over to Linda. 'I'm not trying to give you a hard time,' she said. 'Really, I'm not. You've been through enough. But you must know what people are saying.' When Linda made no response, she continued. 'They're saying that you're applying double standards.'

Linda frowned. 'In what sense?'

'Well, they say that what you're implying with your decision is that men are allowed to get away with cheating but women aren't. That men aren't held accountable in the same way that women are.'

'I see.' Linda was silent for a moment. She sat down in front of the computer. 'I've got work to catch up on,' she said. Then, raising her head, she spoke rapidly, not looking directly at Delia. 'I don't know how to explain it to you, Delia,' she said. 'I don't mind your questions, because you're a good friend. But I don't know how to answer them. All I can tell you is that it's got nothing whatsoever to do with expecting less from men and more from women. Nothing at all.'

'Then what's it got to do with?'

She paused. 'Loyalty.'

'But they've both been disloyal.'

'I know ... but, as I said before, it's not the same.'

'Why not? I want to understand.' Delia got up and took the cups to the sink to wash them.

'Because ...' Her eyes filled suddenly with tears and she had difficulty in seeing the computer screen in front of her. She scarcely understood her own words as they tumbled from her mouth. 'It's because ... because Pam chose *me*.'

Later, she thought about her response. Delia had not had the faintest idea what she meant when she said, 'because Pam chose *me*'. And how could she? It was absurd to expect anyone to understand such an enigmatic utterance. But it was the only answer she was able to give.

The truth was that she could not account rationally for her actions. There was no good reason she could give – even to herself – for why she was still married to Jon, cooking his dinners, sharing his bed; yet she had had no contact with her sister for almost a year, and was determined never to speak to her again. Her choices had their origins in a realm in which there were no explanations, no justifications; only echoes and memories, soft yet powerful stirrings amid the shadows of recondite days.

She walked from room to room. It was growing dark, but she didn't put on any lights. Twilight made the house look different: new shapes emerged, beckoning to one another across the empty spaces. She'd been living there for years, but of late she felt like an interloper.

'This will never, ever leave me,' she said again to herself. She couldn't get it out of her head. That was what the American soldier in Afghanistan had said: *this will never, ever leave me*. And then, suddenly, she knew why it had sounded so familiar. The elusive memory came out of its hiding-place and disclosed itself. Of course! They were her own words, her assurance to herself as she walked back with Pam to the Mollers' farmhouse. How odd that those six words – uttered in so far removed a context – should transport her to that time.

In the recollection of that moment, the afternoon at the farm came back to her, as clearly as if it were yesterday: the fading autumn sunlight, the wind which grew colder and colder as the sun set, the mournful creak of the windmill, the stench of the rotten egg as it trickled down her neck. These were not merely memories: they were the beginnings of events which were still playing themselves out; which still had their course to run. They had conspired together to create a place she could never leave. Everything that had happened lately was urging her back, winding and rewinding the coils of time, looping them about her.

It began that day at the Moller farm. And what made it possible was the surpassing moment when the gift of loyalty had been bestowed on her; when Pam chose her, the stinking little sister, and turned her back on the twins. It had meant everything to her. It still meant everything to her. It was a promise that came from the very heart of staunchness, where one was safe forever.

And that was what she couldn't forgive. She could never forgive Pam – not for breaking such a promise, but for making it in the first place.

There was a time when loyalty gave the answer.

That time had not passed.

And the answer was the same.

Recognition

When I saw the envelope in which the invitation came, I thought it might be a request for an interview. I still get those occasionally, although fewer and fewer as time goes by. People nowadays don't want to ask me about Kobus and about those years as they did after he died. They think he belongs too much to the past. And I too have become something left over from the past. Let me tell you, that is a sad fate. This has become a young country now, and whether people are pleased about it or fighting against it, that is where their energies lie. Those who do try to recall the past want it to be tough and aggressive. That is certainly not my style. Besides, I am an old lady. I lead a quiet life and would not have it otherwise, but there is still a part of me that does not like to be forgotten; and because I have a responsibility towards Kobus's memory, I would not like him and what he accomplished to be forgotten either. That is understandable. There is a kind of loyalty that must be suspicious of things that are new.

I thought also that it might be an invitation to attend a political rally of the Party. Sometimes I am invited to participate in those sorts of gatherings. I find it hard to refuse, because I know that they want me there to represent Kobus and I suppose they are the last people who still cherish all that he fought for. Yet it is difficult for me to know what to do, for I feel that the Party is no longer the one that he represented so loyally, and that he would not approve of some of the directions it has chosen. Also, I am not a political person myself, even though I was the wife of the Prime Minister for a number of years. Politics was Kobus's life and, of course, I supported him in every way that I could. But if he had remained a lawyer or I had married a schoolteacher like myself, I would have been quite contented. Politics is a rough business and I am not a rough person. As a child, I did not even like competitive games. Then I found myself having to support Kobus in the most competitive game of all. But I did what was needed and perhaps even more than was needed. I shirked nothing, no matter how unpleasant. I do not say this because I expect praise or gratitude. I say it simply because that is how it was. I must insist on the truth of what was. People are not satisfied with changing the present nowadays, they want to change the past too. I feel I have to protect what I know. I have become strangely jealous of my own life.

Anyway, I tore the envelope open. At first I thought it must be a joke or a trick that someone was playing on me, for I really was never so astonished in my life. I had been so isolated and so removed from what is happening in politics, despite the courtesies extended to me by the Party, that I didn't know that such a gathering was even being planned. And it is the last thing I would ever have imagined likely. The present government could not possibly be favourably disposed towards me – that is, if they ever gave me a thought. Yet, if this was not a hoax, I was being invited to a luncheon at the residence of the President.

I was distrustful. I didn't want to do anything that would make me feel regret afterwards. I didn't want to be used by any group of people for their own political ends, except by the Party, who usually use me very respectfully; and even then I am not entirely happy about it. I am cautious by nature and being married to Kobus for all those years has made me even more so, for he was a careful and scrupulous man, and he taught me a great deal. He taught me more as a father teaches his child than as a man teaches his wife. And I knew so little, even though I had been to the Teacher's Training College. But what I learned I have kept with me all my life, for where else does stability lie?

The only way I could establish whether or not it was a joke was to phone up Magdalena. If I received an invitation, then she must have received one too, I thought; and she is more in touch with what is happening politically at the moment than I am. I worked out that there were six widows of former prime ministers or presidents still living. But Magdalena was the only one I could speak to. The husbands of two of them were bitter rivals of Kobus. The third one's husband betrayed him terribly, even though they studied together at the University of the Orange Free State and were allies for many years after that. Kobus never forgave him and the quarrel went on until the day Kobus died. The fourth widow has Alzheimer's disease – they say she doesn't even recognise her own children.

Magdalena said that it was a genuine invitation. The President wishes to make peace with the past, she said; this is his way of showing that reconciliation can take place. She sounded very excited about it. She was certainly going to attend the luncheon and she urged me to attend it too. I said that I would think about it. Magdalena always loved feeling important; that is one of her little failings. Her husband died in office and so she lost him and the public attention at the same time. I do not condemn her for being that way, but I am different. Even when Kobus was Prime Minister, I did not exploit the powerful position that circumstances had given me, although I worked hard and carried out my duties conscientiously. I like to think that, as a result, I was a dignified and thoughtful presence and a good role model for women generally, not only for those whose husbands were in politics.

Magdalena said that she had already established that the other widows, except for poor Mrs Havenga, were willing to accept the President's invitation. She told me that Mrs Havenga just sits and stares blankly. It is pitiful to see. Her husband had the largest majority in parliament ever achieved in the history of the Party and she remembers nothing of it. All those triumphs are lost to her. She also told me that Mrs Groenewald had not been well, she had had a hip replacement last year and other health problems, but she was very excited about the invitation and determined to attend the luncheon. I said politely that I was glad she was feeling up to it; I didn't think it was necessary to remind Magdalena about the great quarrel between Kobus and Jan Groenewald.

Was Magdalena sure that accepting the invitation was the right thing to do, I asked? Was it *politically* the right thing to do? Of course, she said. The President was recognising our importance and the importance of our late husbands. It would be good for the morale of the people who still believed in the old values to see the President extending such recognition and courtesy to us. We owed it to those people. They were in such despair. Their culture was under attack. They struggled to get jobs because of Affirmative Action. They had become outcasts in their own land. Before I put the phone down I said that I would accept the invitation. I still had some reservations, but I kept them from Magdalena. She was thrilled. Every widow would now be coming, she said; except, of course, for poor Mrs Havenga.

You cannot imagine how strange it felt to enter the official residence again after all those years. People feel uncomfortable even when they have cause to enter a house which they once lived in; imagine, then, how disconcerting it was for me to enter the residence where I once, as the Prime Minister's wife, entertained important people from all over the world – Taiwan, Chile, Paraguay. Now I entered as the guest of a man whom my husband fought to keep out of it. It was so difficult for me that I had to think deliberately about my pride before I went in – how much pride I would wear, how I would wear it. It was almost like deciding how to arrange a scarf. The taxi dropped me off and I walked slowly and deliberately, carrying myself without haughtiness but rather as I felt a woman should who is conscious all the time of a solemn duty. I wanted to be worthy of that important thing that had been entrusted to me and that others, despite their own importance, were prepared to recognise in me.

Magdalena was ahead of me and I could already see that she was not behaving in a dignified manner. The President himself was receiving her at the door and she was gushing over him, not permitting him even to complete his words of welcome. There was something cringing about her, I thought; a smallness in her gratitude. I felt ashamed of her behaviour. I was determined that there would be nothing to be ashamed of in my behaviour. Someone who was standing near the President approached me and I told him who I was. He returned to the President with the information and then the President came towards me, smiling and greeting me. I shook his hand firmly. I said I was pleased to be there. I thanked him for the invitation. That was all. I was ushered into the dining hall.

It looked very different from the room that I had known, the room that I had redecorated myself a few months after Kobus became Prime Minister. The colours were bolder. We had painted the walls a light salmon colour, but now they were reddish brown with a white border. Not one work of art that we had chosen was still there, not even the Pierneef or the Van Wouw sculpture. Why was it necessary to remove those? The Pierneef was a landscape, the Van Wouw was a torso – there was nothing political about them. In a strange way, the sight of this redecorated room affected me more than all the other changes I had seen, such as watching the President being sworn in or the generals from the army and the air force saluting a black man.

Of course, I showed none of the emotion that I felt. I looked around to see where I had been seated. Before I could find the card with my name on it, Magdalena was pointing it out to me and waving at me. It was not too near to her, thankfully, nor too near to Mrs Groenewald, who was making a point of ignoring my presence. The seats on either side of me were still empty. A waiter stepped forward immediately to offer me a drink. I chose soda water, as I always do.

Gradually the table began to fill up. There were a number of black women, whom I was surprised to see there. Then I realised that it was a gathering of political widows of all sorts, including the widows of people who had fought against the previous government. Black women and white women were being seated next to one another. The woman on my left was an Indian woman. She introduced herself, but her name was not familiar to me. The one on my right greeted me, but did not introduce herself, so I did not tell her who I was either. I tried to glance at her name card, but it was angled towards her and

I could not read it. After that she sat quietly, making no attempt to speak to me or anyone else. She was a young woman, much younger than most of the other women there. She was perhaps less than forty years old.

When the President came into the room, we stood up. He asked us all to sit down. Then he made a short speech. He was honoured to receive us all; he was delighted that we had come. This was a time of reconciliation and dialogue, and we were all participating in that by sitting down to dine together, some of us bitter foes in the past, and showing the country that such things were possible. Then he spoke of those few who were not there, whose health had prevented them from coming. He named them all and said that he would call on them soon. He even mentioned Mrs Havenga, and I wondered whether he knew what condition she was in. He named two women who had managed to come despite recent health problems of a serious nature, and thanked them in particular. One of them was Mrs Groenewald.

Then the President sat down and they began to serve the meal. There was a cold cucumber soup, followed by saddle of venison. Television cameras had been set up and it was strange to think that we were being filmed as we ate. The Indian lady turned to me repeatedly, happy to make small talk, and we spoke about the food and about the President's speech. She pointed out some of the women and told me who they were and I did the same for her, pointing out and identifying each of the widows from the former government. The black woman on the other side remained very uncommunicative. If I spoke to her, she answered briefly, but made no effort to contribute to the conversation of her own accord, so I gave up and spoke to the Indian lady all the time. While the dessert was being served, the President got up and began to move around the table, speaking to each of the women. I could see Magdalena clasping his hand and looking up at him, speaking at length while the television cameras and microphones were focused upon her. I was pleased that I could not hear what she was saying.

When the President got to our part of the table, the Indian lady sprang up and they hugged each other. They clearly knew each other well. The President enquired after members of her family, they spoke of mutual friends and acquaintances. Then he moved on to me. He spoke to me with great courtesy. He knew that I had two daughters and he enquired after them. He asked me about my health. He wished to know where I lived. Did I enjoy my retirement from the pressures of political life? Not particularly, I said; it was a duty that one assumed without question and gave up when the time was over.

It occurred to me, as we spoke, that he is two years older than I. He was kindly, polite, yet somehow distant in a way that I could not quite put my finger on. His eyes are more inscrutable than the photographs suggest. I was not very pleased with my responses; I felt they were a little ungracious. I wanted to do more than thank him for inviting me to the luncheon. I wanted to thank him for the gesture, for the symbolism. I know the importance of symbolism, for our own culture is full of symbols. But I didn't know how to do so without gushing like Magdalena, without yielding something up to him that I was supposed to keep from him. So I was formal, polite in my turn and controlled. He passed on.

When he greeted by name the black woman next to me, I felt startled. I drank some soda water to hide my reaction. Hearing that name again, the name that had vexed Kobus for so many years and even after he retired from political life, the name that had been linked to his throughout the world, was a shock to me. That name had first begun to inconvenience us before Kobus was Prime Minister – it was when he was still Minister of Justice. And when he became Prime Minister, journalists and other people hostile to the government referred whenever they could to those suicides and accidents that occurred while people were in police custody; and always they referred, in particular, to the death of this woman's husband. And perhaps, as Kobus admitted to me, some of them were caused by police exceeding their duties, for those were trying times, and in trying times people are not always at their best. But it didn't mean that Kobus had anything to do with it. He was a fair man, firm but always fair. And it grieved him that his name should be linked to such events and I grieved with him, for I was protective of his reputation as, indeed, I still am.

Yet here was the widow of the most notorious of all those detainees, the one whose death caused an international outcry. I had been sitting next to her throughout the luncheon and I had not known who she was. Now, after the President moved on from us to speak to another group of ladies, we looked at each other and were silent. Her silence made me very uncomfortable. I felt the need to say something, something appropriate to the occasion, but it was difficult to know what to say.

Finally I said, 'I'm sorry, I didn't know who you were.'

'I knew who you were,' she said. We sat silently again. She bent her head to her dessert. It was clear that, if any gestures were to be made, they would have to come from me.

'The President has done a great thing,' I said. 'He has brought us together so that we can make peace with the past and recognise our common humanity. After all, we are all widows. Each of us has suffered a loss.'

She looked up again and seemed to stare at something behind me, something in the far distance.

'Is that what you have come to do – to make peace with the past?' she asked.

I thought for a while before I answered. 'No,' I said. If there was one gesture I could make, it was to tell her the truth. It was a relief to do so. 'I came to make sure that no one is going to take the past away from me.'

When I said that, she blinked and looked directly at me. It was impossible to know what to make of the expression on her face. Only someone who knew her well could have interpreted it, and I didn't know her at all.

'Perhaps we have something in common after all,' she said.

Afterword: Observations on Post-apartheid Literature

There has been much debate recently about the state of South African literature. Literary critics concur that the imperatives that fashioned protest and resistance writing from the 1950s until the 1980s were ameliorated, or at least differently inflected, following the advent of democracy in 1994. While writers had responded to the pressing realities of apartheid injustice – social realism was the preferred mode and much of the literature was characterised by what Louise Bethlehem refers to as 'a rhetoric of urgency'[1] – the post-apartheid dispensation was a new context for composition, with its own priorities and demands.

Iain Sinclair, in his peripatetic portrait of London, warns us against cartography:

> We have to recognise the fundamental untrustworthiness of maps: they are always pressure group publications. They represent special pleading on behalf of some quango with a subversive

> agenda, something to sell. Maps are a futile compromise between information and knowledge.[2]

It is premature to begin mapping the post-apartheid literary terrain: we are not yet in a position to extricate ourselves from the field, and to achieve an overview of its contours and features. In a recent article, Leon de Kock laments that the literary scene in South Africa since its transition from apartheid has been the subject of only limited scholarly attention.[3] There is, he suggests, a 'bewildering array of new names [which] has literally taken over from the older local canon of Schreiner, Smith, Fugard, Brutus, Mphahlele, Gordimer, Coetzee, Dangor, Mda et al.'[4] In order to produce any general description, detailed critical work needs first to be conducted which comes to terms with this proliferation. What follows in this brief account is not, therefore, a map. It is a series of speculations which might afford additional insights into the stories of David Medalie, and their context.

It could be argued that much of the fiction published in the first decade of democracy implicitly or explicitly engaged the logic of the Truth and Reconciliation Commission (TRC). Most short stories, novels and memoirs were driven by the idea that we needed to salvage repressed histories and create opportunities for the previously-silenced to speak. The TRC functioned in much of this writing as a conceit; an organising trope for elaborating our relationship with history, as well as for forging a path towards that elusive (and now strangely anachronistic) notion, 'the New South Africa'. It would have seemed almost churlish for writers not to embrace the transformative potential of the Commission, and so many raised their voices in support of the unifying aspirations of the post-apartheid dispensation.

Confession, or at least the acknowledgment of complicity, came to dominate white writing, as if each author was facing 'the perpetrator within', and, through a forensic examination of his or her actions and conscience, seeking expiation. As is not uncommon with such noble intentions, many authors, particularly those representing apartheid childhoods, seemed to be indulging nostalgia as much as they were orientated to a genuinely reconciled future. Redress – even imaginative redress – in a divided society is never a simple matter. In some of these novels and short stories, as protagonists wax lyrical about the importance of their domestic workers in their upbringing, they betray with deepest consequence their attachment to that world (of sunny skies, long days at the pool, and a brother on the border) which made of domestic work what it actually was.

Black authors, who inclined with a few notable exceptions to autobiography and memoir rather than fiction, sought to set the record straight: to tell those stories of resistance and suffering that apartheid ideologues had repressed or corrupted. Some of these works traded in the 'authenticity' of their authors; their legitimacy was assured by the lives lived by activists and politicians, rather than the creativity with which they were rendered. There are important exceptions, though; carefully balanced works of reflection that do credit to the impulse to expose the moral, political and emotional entanglements of the past. For these writers, the TRC uncapped a wellspring of possibility, and it was rejuvenating, as perhaps no other South African social or political institution has ever been.

The transition from apartheid was, of course, accompanied by the end of decades of separation and isolation. First, the influx of black South Africans into the cities in the course of the laissez-faire greying process of the early 1990s and the limited movement of middle-class black South Africans into previously white areas brought people into a proximity never before experienced. After 1994, a staggering influx of African migrants occurred from, among other countries, Nigeria, the Democratic Republic of the Congo, Cameroon and Zimbabwe. In apartheid discourse, 'Africa' was always elsewhere (a sign on military campaign maps or on charts detailing corporate strategy): now it was brought home – became home. At the same time as this Africanisation unfolded, South Africa – freed from boycotts and sanctions – became, in certain respects, global. We shifted rapidly from being the world's pariah state to being the premier destination for political and ethical tourists and scholars. We became a context in which it was possible to brush up against hope. All of these changes combined to disseminate and diversify the trope of the TRC. The notion of a 'national literature' was cogent and relatively settled under conditions of isolation. The transitional post-apartheid dispensation began to beg questions. Who, for instance, in the face of endless arrivals and departures is placed to tell South African stories? Are some stories more 'authentic', others more in keeping with the priorities of reconciliation? What classifies as South African literature?

It is possible to discern, probably since about 2000, a shift in our literatures, as the lived realities of the post-apartheid dispensation – contests of power within the government of liberation, the full exposure of the HIV/Aids epidemic, the upsurge in crime and corruption, the brutality of xenophobia, and the failure of aspects of the central bureaucracy – began to settle in. What has happened since the TRC conceit began to loosen its hold on the literary imagination, and as literary culture began to be organised along different lines of emigration, diaspora and migration? What, too, has been the implication of the new politics of publishing? Let me speculate on just four related matters.

Firstly, when we consider the literary institution we need to take account of the transnational mobility of many of our contemporary writers: several of those who are integral to 'our' literature no longer live here, or come and go. Their writing is 'South African' at various removes, with distinct affiliations to other contexts and literary traditions. Much of this debate has been galvanised by the career of J.M. Coetzee, in particular his decision to emigrate to Australia. (In some respects, *Disgrace* seems a watershed text: it announces the end of the optimism of the TRC, and ushers in an era of unrelenting moral and epistemological complexity.) But there are other examples of South African writers who live elsewhere most of the time: Anne Landsman, Zakes Mda, Elleke Boehmer, Eben Venter, Breyten Breyentenbach, Justin Cartwright, and Christopher Hope, to name a few. This mobility begs the question – which preoccupies the judges of literary awards every year – as to how one decides on the nationality of an author. One is also driven to ponder what is at stake in this debate. What are the politics of national ownership when it comes to authors and texts, and from whence does this anxiety about the 'impurity' of our literature derive? South Africans, for an array of reasons, have always invested strongly in the notion that individuals – authors, actors, athletes, leaders – are 'ours'. Neither the constituency to which they might belong, nor the dynamics of claiming ownership are as clear or settled as they might once have seemed.

In parallel with the mobility of writers caught up in these various pathways, is the energetic transculturalism of the present. The nation, Benedict Andersen[5] and others have shown us, is an imagined entity, usually wielded strategically in the interests of a particular political constituency. The imagination, our projective sense of the poetic and its relation to the cultural, is far more fluid and fluent than any such nationalist singularity can countenance. Thought and writing, in a world of constant and variegated exchanges, does not respect borders or boundaries. It is even feasible to argue that the most creative works in contemporary South African literature are those that range most widely, are the most uninhibited and experimental, and the most willing to give up a proprietary sense of 'national' story-telling.

Secondly, it can be argued that the relationship between the political and the personal in South African fiction has shifted. While writers continue to engage issues of social and economic injustice, many are centrally concerned with the interiority of their characters, their relationships and their lived experience. It would be banal to suggest that significant South African writing ever neglected the individual and personal; it is, except in the cases of the most pedantic socialist realism or brittle allegory, impossible to reflect oppression and the prospect of liberation other than through the lens of subjectivity. But the balance has shifted: contemporary writers need not apologise for emphasising the inward turn of their characters, rather than the march of history or the crushing realities of exploitation. The private has gained in legitimacy, and with it a new range of existential, emotional and even spiritual preoccupations.

Thirdly, post-TRC publishing reflects a marked turn to, and investment in, generic writing, with a particular emphasis on popular genres. Crime-writing, chick-lit, satire, and so on, have burgeoned, many of which texts are as influenced by international publishing trends, writerly conventions and readers' expectations as they are by any received sense of a 'national literature'. I have heard many writers express the opportunity of this generic affiliation as liberation from the narrow expectations of anti-apartheid writing, which many experienced as overdetermining. Loren Kruger[6] refers to aspects of post-apartheid culture as 'post-anti-apartheid', which accurately describes a reorientation in terms of priorities other than the political.

This begs the question, though, as to whether we are witnessing, in this new worldliness, the maturation of the post-apartheid literary scene or a dilution that will make South African literature at once more global, but also less individuated, less discernible and, perhaps, less significant. We are inclined, in the wake of apartheid's draconian controls, to assume that globalisation is inherently beneficial. What, though, might we lose if phrases like 'South African Literature' and 'a South African author' ceased to function as assertions of particularity and difference? What would this loss mean for local authors and readers, but also for publishing and distribution?

My final observation is the most important, but also the most contentious. In some respects at least, contemporary South African writing might be described (although the grounds for disagreeing with this contention are obvious) as 'post-ideological'. Anti-apartheid writing, as well as writing of the transition to a democratic order, was fuelled by a version of the nation, and of nation-building.

Novelists, poets and short-story writers are now willing to countenance far greater ambivalence about the claims of nationalism, about the murky depths of our various histories and about the utopian schemes and dystopian fears that dominated our past. We are, it seems, currently in the muddy middle-ground typical of all postcolonial states, perhaps of all states, facing a range of both particular and shared demands and challenges. It is this complicated territory that Craig MacKenzie and Ronit Frenkel describe as 'post-transitional', which is, I will argue, a compromised term.[7]

This 'middle-ground' might be understood, to use a different metaphor taken from the story 'Crowd Control' in this collection, as living on a mezzanine. Prior to the liberation of South Africa, writers were haunted by a sense of approaching catastrophe and inspired by the hope for liberation. We lived, the dominant literary ideology asserted, in what Antonio Gramsci called an 'interregnum': the old was dying but the new could not be born.[8] What remained for authors in the context of this crisis was to put their shoulders to the wheel of history. In a sense, this logic – of being subsumed by historical process and necessity – continued through the first decade of democracy. For most authors, though, this teleological rumbling forward is no longer an option: many reflect instead lives caught in-between an old order that has – quite rightly, and to the relief of all right-thinking individuals – disappeared, and the uncertainties of the future.

In the watershed year of 1994, the South African anthropologist Robert Thornton observed, in an article published in *Anthropology Today*, that it 'has always seemed that South Africa was on the brink of collapse'.[9] At each historical horizon, given the contesting realities contained in its borders and its long history of violence, there has been a pervasive 'sense that it could never work, yet somehow must work'. This has led to a unique political and existential condition: 'a constant sense of suspense'. The apocalyptic threat of a 'bloody and final conflict' resides deep within the South African psyche. Thornton, facing the advent of democracy in South Africa, suggested a contrary mindset: that we should interpret 'transition' (the transcendental signifier of the post-apartheid dispensation) not as teleology, not as a journey to 'a final state', but as a permanent condition, not unlike 'Trotsky's idea of a permanent revolution'.

This habitation, this 'constant sense of suspense' – which, at the risk of pretension, we might call a 'mezzanine ontology' – suggests that we are denied the symmetry and clarity of progression; that we are caught up in a world of contradictions and ironies, and that the actual struggle we have to engage is to find a unifying purpose in a world of complexity and difference. One could argue that this makes South Africans' lives much like those lived elsewhere by everyone. But our mezzanine is distinctly our own: the world we have left below and the one above us, the lived experience of which we cannot yet discern, are fundamentally local, even as we come to acknowledge that they are simultaneously transnational and translatable.

This seeming contradiction – that our habitus is both overwhelmingly distinct and distinctly shared – remains key to understanding what it means to live and write as a South African. There is much that only those who have shared our awful history will understand, but it is incumbent on us to communicate, from that particularity, a condition of suspension that is common to many people in diverse contexts.

It seems to me that it is in their delicate, finely-crafted articulation of this in-between condition that David Medalie's stories gain much of their power. It is complex to represent lives caught in a faltering, hesitant logic and temporality, while also capturing the resilience and optimism entailed in individual choice. The stories tack between the national mezzanine and the lineaments of subjectivity in ways that place them among the most significant portraits of South African life and living now.

In some respects, the modernist short story (and I am thinking here particularly of the narrative modes of James Joyce, Joseph Conrad, Virginia Woolf and E.M. Forster) might be particularly suited to our present, just as other modes of the short story were appropriate to our past. The smaller canvas of the genre compels an author to devise situations and moments of interiority (recognition, resignation, hope or aspiration) that distil the swirling realities of the world. At their best, modernist short stories are never pedantic; they never resolve the matters they raise, but rather leave both their characters and readers suspended on the brink of a recognition that remains – for all of its powerful implications – somewhat inchoate, just out of reach. In a transitional context like ours, in which most of us experience the world as difficult to read, this hesitation, this modest authorial purview, seems entirely apt. As we all struggle in a period that might be described as entailing a 'crisis of thinking and being', we might justifiably turn, as David Medalie does, to the practices of composition suited to comparable times of intellectual and political upheaval and complication.

Medalie is masterful at leading his characters and us, as readers, towards understanding, but also at withholding the consolations of certainty that would make the world comfortably legible and, hence, anodyne. We are left suspended – as we are.

Michael Titlestad
University of the Witwatersrand, Johannesburg

Notes

1 Bethlehem, Louise. 2006. *Skin Tight: Apartheid Literary Culture and its Aftermath.* Pretoria: UNISA Press, pp.1–20.

2 Sinclair, Iain. 1997. *Lights Out for the Territory: Nine Excursions in the Secret History of London.* London: Granta. p.142.

3 De Kock, Leon. 2008. 'A History of Restlessness: And Now for the Rest'. *English Studies in Africa* 51(1): pp.109–22.

4 De Kock, 'A History of Restlessness', p.115.

5 Anderson, Benedict. 2006. *Imagined Communities: Reflections on the Origin and Spread of Nationalism.* London: Verso.

6 Kruger, Loren. 2002. '"Black Atlantics", "White Indians" and "Jews": Locations, Locutions and Syncretic Identities in the Fiction of Dangor and Others'. *Scrutiny2* 7(2): pp.34–50.

7 MacKenzie, Craig and Frenkel, Ronit, eds. Forthcoming 2010. *English Studies in Africa: Special Issue – Post-transitional South African Literature* 53(1).

8 Gramsci, Antonio. 1971. *Selections from the 'The Prison Notebooks' of Antonio Gramsci*. London: Lawrence and Wishart, p.87.

9 Thornton, Robert. 1994. 'South Africa: Countries, Boundaries, Enemies and Friends'. *Anthropology Today* 10(6): pp.7–15.